"My Life, Made Possible By Pop Culture"

A ...TBD Production

Written (and Lived) By Danielle Turchiano

ISBN: 1453635432
ISBN-13: 9781453635438

*To **my mother**, who just wanted me to be happy above anything else.*

INTRODUCTION

When I was a kid, my mother tried to impart a rule of no more than two hours of television each night. I say "tried" instead of simply "had" because she worked such hellish hours that she was never home to enforce such a thing. And if my father couldn't even master making a green vegetable along with every dinner the way she asked him to, there was no way he was going to be able to handle this, either.

My mother's reasoning was that she didn't want television to "rot my brain" through its biased and oftentimes negative propaganda... but also through the radiation. My mother was greatly afraid of the radiation through televisions, computers, and microwaves, and would not even allow the latter into the house. That little known fact is somewhat sad and ironic, considering she needed similar radiation to zap a tumor years later. But I digress.

I used to fight my mother on this television rule just about every single time that she would bring it up. I needed to keep it on, I would argue, to keep me company in the afternoons when I got home from school. I needed it on during dinner to immerse myself in other families— ones that weren't screaming at each other over dry pieces of chicken and no green vegetables. I needed it on in the early hour of the night, providing a soundtrack while I poured over my math or science workbooks. In fact, I would often try to plead my case, when I get called upon in class to recite a fact from one such workbook, I could often recall said fact simply by remembering the scene that was on the television screen while I was reading it. I was a situational learner. Or something.

I didn't notice it then— or even when I first sat down to begin writing the stories and chapters herein— but my mother was right. Television may not have rotted my brain completely (I went to a magnet high school, did respectfully well on the SATs, and attended a prestigious university, at which I made the Dean's List—all while still studying television (oh okay, and some film) I might add!), but it definitely messed me up in one very key way. Through its couples, television set ridiculous and seemingly unreasonable expectations for any romantic relationship I might encounter in the so-called "real world." And though I should have been smart enough to say "It's just TV" through it all, I placed a much greater weight on everything I saw— and learned— there.

Despite growing up in a household that only featured the seven-channel options of rabbit ears' television, I still managed to spend the better part of the 1990s learning my life lessons by watching fictional characters experience them. Using Zack & Kelly, Jesse & Rebecca, and Monica & Chandler as my guides for what strong, successful couples were supposed to look like, I set out, perhaps a bit misguided, to find a suitor of my own that would fit nicely into the mold countless sitcoms carved out for me. But something went horribly awry, and I was forced to come to terms with the fact that all I looked to when I was a child to tell me what real life could be was, in fact, perhaps only relevant for a *reel* life.

Of course once you start, it is not easy to stop looking to television for your own life lessons: they're just so readily accessible when they come into your home with just the touch of a button! So needless to say mine is a true tale, but it is also somewhat of a cautionary one.

My mother passed away from cancer before she had the chance to finish reading this manuscript—let alone read my printed admission that she was right. Sometimes I wonder if she had spent more time sitting in front of the television with me, if some of the things we watched would have spurred conversations and given another frame of reference for the beliefs I was developing. Sometimes I wonder if the waves of radiation from the set could have killed any cancerous cells that were trying to take her over. But mostly I just wonder what she would think about the fact that so much of who I am—for better and for worse—is made up of bits and pieces from television from my childhood.

Though this is very clearly not the life she may have dreamed for me, I hope she would at least be proud that I took an obsessive hobby and turned it into a (hopefully long-term and profitable) career. As you will learn from the pages forthcoming, I still have to work on relationships later.

FADE IN:

INT. MODERN LIVING ROOM – DAY

A mother and her daughter sit on a wooden floor playing with Barbie dolls. The daughter stops pensively and looks at her mother with hope in her eyes.

DAUGHTER

Hey, Ma, how do you know when it's true love?

MOTHER

Usually you make the music louder. And you can move in on them. Or sometimes they look up in slow-motion.

The daughter rolls her eyes.

DAUGHTER

No, not on TV; in real life.

The mother's face clouds over, and she gazes off in the distance, eager to find something to which to change the subject. She doesn't have a clue as to how to answer and guide her child through this tough time in her life, so she finds it easier just to ignore the issue. Her own personal examples only come from those fictional television couples, and she knows from firsthand experience how unhealthy it can be to grow up with *those* as role models. So the two just sit in silence.

FADE OUT.

I should probably "open" by admitting I consider myself the star of a television series about my life...the only problem is that if my life actually *were* a television show, it would most likely get canceled after one or two episodes. Nothing really interesting ever happens to me—unless you count the stuff that goes on within my own head. So why, then, would my life warrant a book, if not a television show? Well, the stuff I mentioned just a second ago that goes on in my own head can be pretty neurotic and crazy, and I have been told that is becoming increasingly popular these days...I have a tendency to obsess and dwell on certain facets of life (not even really *my* life, but the general collective life in general), and these are things that keep me from going about "normally."

By the way, these admissions now only serve to explain the "I told you so" that will come at the end.

If such a scene as the one that I mentioned a few short words ago appeared in a work of fiction, as it did in Amy Heckerling's *I Could Never Be Your Woman,*[1] it would have that slightly unreal quality about it that inevitably causes me to laugh-out-loud even if I slightly roll my eyes while doing so. In fact, I don't so much merely laugh as I do snort. However, should a similar event occur in my actual life, I might just have a panic attack. Like Michelle Pfeiffer's character in that aforementioned movie, I'd have to take a moment to pause and figure out a way to distract my child from the fact that I can't quite answer, and if I'm honest enough to say that I don't know, I'll inevitably have to contend with the "*But why?*" that follows.

Now, I should probably preface this by explaining that I don't plan to have my own children, and in choosing that route, I also plan to check the Boys Only box on the adoption application...but that's really a whole can of worms onto itself, and perhaps we'll get to it later. Not having girls, in my opinion, should alleviate some of

1 A brilliantly funny romantic comedy that sadly went straight-to-DVD and deserves to be added to your Netflix queue Right. Now.

the past experiences that I'd be expected to share, but I know I, too, won't be able to stave off *all* of the questions forever.

Now, don't get me wrong; it's not that I don't know what love is. I sang "Be My Girl" and "Please Don't Go Girl" at the top of my high-pitched lungs, making my voice crack in all of the right emotional places with the rest of my fellow tween girls. I sat with my chin in my hands, perched on the edge of the couch, my short legs sticking to the plastic covering with sweat and humidity, watching a bleached blond Zack Morris pursue the cheerleader of his dreams. Somehow I knew— even when he didn't seem to— that they would end up together; through all of the other girlfriends (whose arcs never spanned much more than a few episodes anyway, fading as metaphorically from his heart as they did from the screen), he always found his way back to the sweet, perky Kelly Kapowski. I was young, and I couldn't quite verbalize it at the time, but somehow in their adolescent, if somewhat naïve, relationship, I found what I believed to be the destiny of true love.

From the very first moments of *Saved By The Bell* (if you ignore the *Miss Bliss* episodes, which I personally do), young Zack was open, honest, and unapologetic for his pursuit of the girl-not-so-literally-next-door. Though they could not have been more different (he was a prankster while she was a goody-goody who never lied to her father; his parents had money and gave him a cellular phone while her father lost his job, causing her to have to miss the prom because she couldn't afford a dress), any minor obstacle thrown at them was shrugged off as being irrelevant and insignificant because all that mattered to them was how they felt about each other.

They were a modern day Romeo and Juliet, which was perhaps a bit too astutely illustrated when they actually went as Romeo and Juliet to one of Bayside's themed dances. And sure, they tested the waters on occasion with others—Kelly had a relationship with a college aged waiter at The Max, and Zack had a string of one episode long relationships (let's ignore a pre-Scientology Leah Remini as the girl he fell for one brief summer, too)—but that just proved they were not some sappy kids who jumped into a relationship and vowed that was it. Quite literally, they were growing up together, and their love matured as they did. They *thought* about it; they saw what else was out there; and they still found their way back to each other. To me, that was true love.

In the beginning, Kelly seemed to be more like an object to Zack, something to obtain like one of his track medals or basketball trophies. When he brought out the life-size cutout of her in a volleyball uniform, their relationship could have very easily started off on a creepy, stalker-like energy, but instead his smile was wide, reflecting genuine infatuation, and his eyes held the kind of puppy love all teenagers long to experience. From there on out it was easy to forgive some of his childish antics and self-sabotaging behavior because it was clear his heart was in the right place. He had the best of intentions, but he was still just a boy dealing with some very adult and therefore complex emotions. He set the bar awfully high for anyone who hoped to follow in his footsteps (and perhaps that is why, in end, Kelly really had no choice but to marry him).

I was in high school before I had my first boyfriend. While the majority of my friends spent the three years of junior high experiencing their first beers and cigarettes and kisses, I was in my room studying. I'd barrel out of the double doors every day promptly at the last bell and power walk straight to the bus stop…and on days it wasn't coming as fast as I needed it to, I'd just power walk the rest of the way home: I was a girl on a mission, and I didn't have any time to waste. I'd get home, grab a snack, and immediately get to work.

In the early years I didn't have a television in my bedroom, as my mother was determined not to allow me more than an hour and a half a night. She thought this could be best regulated by keeping only one set in the house, in the living room, where I would have to fight for the remote with my out-of-work father who would surely pull rank on me the majority of the time. Still, I managed to use my cunning wiles to get my way (and my channel) by presenting the option of either allowing me to watch my cartoons or whatever or he'd have to engage in a game of Barbies or Sorry!, which I knew were his two least favorite things. Needless to say, the television was always cool and dark when I got home from school, just waiting for me to turn it on and put it to good use. And so I did.

This had been a ritual from practically as far back in my young life as I can remember, and as I sat in front of the television for five or six (or eight or ten) hours a day, I was not just one of those kids who liked background noise while doing homework: I was studying the television instead. In fact, I very rarely did any actual homework in front of it at all, though I often had textbooks open and strewn across the floor, and in later years, my bed, to make it *look* like I was working on something a bit more acceptably scholarly.

But no, I was merely fascinated, not only by the pretty people, but also by the way stories were told— how lighting, shot design, movement, editing, and facial expressions all enhanced the plot and often unrealistically expositional dialogue. It became an outlet for me to learn about creativity before I tried to produce my own. I never passed out comatose on the couch the way many did—just letting the television wash over them. Every textbook on my required reading list in film school clearly separated the passive viewing of television to the active viewing of films: people have to leave their homes—or so was the theory decades ago when it was formed—to see a film, so audiences have to have something invested in them to make the effort. Television, however, is in our own home, so we can multitask when watching and only pay half-attention to what's on the screen. But I concentrated *all* of my attention on the programs; I ate that shit up! And I found friends in the characters, whether they were the precocious farm animals of *Tiny Toons* or the older brother and sister types of *Saved by the Bell*.

Eventually, though, my childhood idols dwindled from the forefront of my consciousness as they were long since taken off the air, and any future they may have still had together was imaginary at best. I began to float in that weird space between childhood and teenager that we have more recently begun to affectionately call "tweendom." No longer was it satisfactory to watch young fictional relationships form; I wanted to be in one of my own. The thing was, I had grown up with afternoon after afternoon of studying other relationships (albeit fictional ones) to get a sense of what I was looking for in one, and I just couldn't trust the boys my age had been doing the same. I was going to have to set my sights on someone more mature, more worldly, and also, just plain older.

JUST ANOTHER SUPERCOUPLE...

The first time I started watching *Days of our Lives* was the summer after sixth grade. My grandmother was very sick and my mother went to stay with her for what felt like a few weeks but was probably only a few days. Every time my mother would make one of those trips, I could tell how bad it was by what she brought me back. One time it was a new Barbie, presented to me when my father and I went to the airport in the middle of the night to pick her up. The time during that summer it was something that, although later proved to be a similar childhood fad to that of the Barbie (or slap bracelets, Tamagatchis, or Pogs), would last a lot longer and shape me in a much more important way.

I didn't really know it at the time, but this trip was the beginning of the end for my grandmother. She had always been in and out of hospitals when I was young, causing me to spend a good portion of my school vacations hanging out in the hallway, learning to fear doctors and nurses and bedpans. My mother had stayed with her in the room all day, sitting by her bedside, watching television, and listening to her breathe more than talk. This time what my mother brought back was her own addiction to a television show, which would soon become mine, as well.

My mother never understood electronics. The first computer we bought was only a tool on which for me to type school papers. Until I went to college, I was the only one in the house using email. Needless to say, even the VCR was a challenge. My mother was still working at the time, but her desire to know what happened on each day's episode overrode that. I ended up taping the episodes for her and then sitting with her at night while she watched them. At first I just waited for them to be over so I could rewind the tape—cueing it up for the next day's recording—but slowly and surely I got into it, too, wanting to know who the characters were, what their relationships to each other were, and why they seemed to be in everlasting doom. Then I *needed* it. I was hooked, but I still couldn't admit it.

See, back about half a dozen years before, I had a friend in elementary school that was ahead of her time; she was undoubtedly the coolest person in my class for many years, though I never would have admitted it back then. She was tall and thin and pretty, and her mom was tall and thin and pretty (and young). Therefore, she was the second generation of cool. She had long curly hair and stylish new clothes every year. Her Halloween costumes were always completely hand-made and unique; one year she came as Peg Bundy from *Married With Children*, a reference lost on those who were not allowed to watch it.[2]

Anyway, my friend's favorite show was *All My Children*, mainly for the romance, she said. She would talk about the tortured lovers as if they were her aunts and uncles, and she was so sophisticated she even cried at things she saw on television. This was something I was teased relentlessly about: no matter what sad movie was shown in assembly— *Bambi* or *Old Yeller* not withstanding— I never even teared up. Maybe I just inherently knew the difference between fiction and reality even back then. Or maybe I was already so jaded that I didn't think the production value was strong enough to warrant such a reaction. A part of me was probably jealous of her, though I couldn't compute such complex emotions at that young, immature age: we were, after all, only six or seven at the time. So just as she sometimes teased me about the clothes I wore, I teased her about her favorite show, saying it was the dumbest, most artificially dramatic form of entertainment. In fact, I told her that as long as I lived,

2 Ironically my parents "banned" a whole hell of a lot of television shows from me when I was growing up, oblivious or just too non-confrontational to realize I would often lie awake listening to my father watching it in the next room over anyway.

I would never watch a soap opera. That's me: putting my foot in my mouth since 1991. I may claim I will never change, but my interests often do.

What drew me so deeply to *DOOL*, as I came to affectionately call the show only about six years later, were the relationships, and once again I came to wish for what I saw on television in my own life. Here were people who would lie, cheat, steal, and kill for each other; here were people who could *survive* lying, cheating, stealing, and killing, and despite it all, could still come out the other side virtually unscathed and still together. The difference here was that I was old enough to recognize the melodrama and to know that certain things were just too great to truly forgive—like when Austin married Sami even though he was really in love with Carrie. Carrie waited—*pining*— as she optimistically assumed he would "sort things out" and come back to her. And he did— it was a flippin' modern day fairytale— but I certainly did not think it was something that should be expected to occur in reality, and I hoped most agreed with me or else countless women would just sit around waiting for their Prince Charming to come rescue them from the dusty interior of their pre-fab apartments. As quickly as I dismissed Carrie's pining, though, I found myself doing the same thing.

Before Jensen Ackles was the snarky, demon-hunting Dean on The CW's cult-favorite *Supernatural,* I fell in love with him as the preppy, blond-locked Eric Brady on *DOOL*. He didn't so much ride into my living room on a white horse as he did sit almost motionless in a red windbreaker on a playground swing, but it didn't matter: the flat studio three-point lighting projected the same halo-esque light on his head, making his angelic face glow and his hazel bedroom eyes sparkle. He had me without even saying a word. Before Jensen, the other guys on television I thought were cute were out of my league: at least a dozen years older and already involved with other people... but Jensen, well he was doable, no?

Heh.

So naturally, when I heard Jensen was doing a personal appearance in New Jersey the day after Valentine's Day 1998, I saw the perfect opportunity to make him start falling in love with me. Tickets were expensive, as far as daily events went, but I honestly didn't think I'd ever get an opportunity like this again. In fact, even after my mother purchased the tickets, I didn't believe I would end up going: I was convinced something terrible would happen to me before the date to prevent it for no real reason other than some good ole fashioned inherited paranoia…but that's really not here nor there right now. All I knew was that this meeting was going to be the official start of my "real" life, and I couldn't risk anything going wrong.

Needless to say, when the day finally came, shock was not the best way to describe how I was feeling—but mix it with elation, euphoria, the biggest high this straight-edge teenager had ever experienced, and you'd be about right. I dressed to look older in a respectable pants suit—*velour* no less; oh yeah, I was classy! But did I mention we were in New Jersey?

I arrived early to the event (just how my mama raised me!), pleased to see my table was just off to the side of the dais where he would sit. I surveyed the merchandise, bought an 8x10 for him to sign, and entered into the raffle. Prizes included being in a photo with him in a magazine, winning dances with him throughout the event, and even getting a personal tour of the set, if you could get yourself out to California. My heart was pounding wildly, but I wouldn't let anyone know it. I like people to think I never get star-struck; actors are just people, too, and they pump their own gas, just like us—at least that's what Us Weekly likes to point out— but that day, I, too, sat with my 35mm SLR poised and ready for his entrance, my purse full of an extra five rolls of film. I'd worry about in what kind of witty banter I should engage him later; in my head it always ended well anyway.

I can't remember the minute-by-minute of the day's events, but I will never forget slipping on the newly polished dance floor when I first entered. I guess my mind fixates on the less than stellar moments, to put it mildly, but I composed myself, didn't fall, and kept going with my head held high. Nothing was going to ruin that day for me. The next thing I remember is the smell of Drakaar Noir (or was it Curve?) that flooded me as I leaned over the photo table, where a company was selling candids of the various stars of different soaps, and a tall man with a deep voice leaned over my shoulder to ask me how it was going. And that was Jensen. And that was his entrance. Low-key and down-to-Earth, which are facets of his personality he has still managed to retain today, even with his elevated level of fame. His mama raised *him* right, too.

I'm not even sure I managed to mumble out a *"Hi,"* but I certainly hope I did.

In fact, I'm not even sure I said *"Hi"* when his rounds brought him to my table, and he slid into a chair straight across from me. I know I smiled widely and tried to lock eye contact the way the couples did on *DOOL* when they had the kind of unresolved feelings for each other that they just couldn't express with words. I'm pretty sure I ended up just looking like a twitchy, nervous fanatic, though; maybe he thought some charity had short-bussed me in for this event as part of a weekly outing or something.

I snapped quite a few photos of the top of his head as he bent over signing 8x10 after 8x10. I know I grinned like an idiot when he wrapped his arm around my chair and posed for a picture. In fact, by the end of the day my jaw hurt from smiling so much, but I couldn't remember saying more than *"I'm Danielle"* to him when he asked to whom he should make out the signed photo. Still, I was convinced that was enough; he would steal glances at me even when he was laughing and chatting at the other tables, even when he was dancing with raffle winners, even when he was eating his dry chicken breast lunch at the dais in the front of the room.

"He'll remember me," I was convinced, "when I show up at the next event. He'll say, "Aren't you...?" And I'll just smile and toss my hair over my shoulder (I ignored the fact I was sporting a bob in those days) and laugh a deep, throaty, mature laugh. He'll invite me to hang out with him in the green room between events, and the rest, as they say (or at least as the journalists at Soap Opera Digest will print) will be history."

Okay, I know I'm babbling like those girls who cry at boy band or *American Idol* concerts, and I'm sorry. I don't know what else to say. First love, when it's right, is often indescribable.

The day in general was a blur, as I spent most of it watching Jensen through my viewfinder like some obsessive-compulsive stalker. I didn't end up dancing with him, but I *did* end up in a group photo that was printed in all of the major soap magazines—my first real claim to fame, though later I would also get a few Letters to the Editor published in Soap Opera Digest and Soap Opera Weekly. I was on my way to becoming a celebrity—even if it was only in my own mind.

And just like those couples on *DOOL*, Jensen and I kept popping up in each other's lives periodically, as if to remind us that we were meant to be together. Granted, I was paying to attend events at which I knew he was scheduled to be, but that's just semantics…or foresight; after all, you can't win the lottery if you don't buy a ticket!

I admit there were times the absence was longer than I would have liked: after he left *DOOL* for bigger stardom and turned up on *Dark Angel*— and though he shined in the program— the subject matter just wasn't for me, so we lived in two separate worlds for a while. Without being able to talk about his work, I'm sad to say we drifted apart even further.

We had our own ups and downs because though I supported his decision to take what he could get to stay a working actor, I always knew he could do better, and I wanted to push him towards roles in which he could be taken more seriously for his talent and not just his smoldering gaze and adorable grin.

So I was in high school before I had my first boyfriend, which may not really be a surprise now that you know to what I was comparing all the barely pubescent boys. And if I'm being completely honest (and I'm really nothing if not *honest*— brutally, embarrassingly honest), it should probably also explain why I broke up with each boyfriend after only a few months. Perhaps a part of me was always holding out for something more, and I figured if one of those guys was *the* one, we'd find our way back just like Jensen and I did. Perhaps ironically, we always did, but when we'd cross paths, it would only be in the halls, on our way to English or Psychology or Calculus.

And just for the record, *yes,* I am well aware that I hold people up to ridiculous standards, and *no,* I am never surprised when most of them can't live up!

VIRTUAL INSANITY...

My First Boyfriend (Trademarked, like My Little Pony...but this accessory came complete not with a hot pink hairbrush but a bright red guitar pick on a string for me to wear around my neck) and I only went on one real date. It was Halloween, and we had a half-day at school, during which I had plans to hang out with two of my closest friends from my neighborhood—or so I thought. When the afternoon bell rang, and I was on my way to the train station, My First Boyfriend crept up behind me and started walking with us, asking us about our plans for the rest of the day. Slowly but surely my two friends pulled back until they had completely disappeared from our eye-line. By that point I had been pretty much ditched—probably premeditatedly—so My First Boyfriend and I went for pizza.

This may not sound like a monumental milestone, but for me it was. See, at the tender age of fourteen, I had pretty much solidified my habits as a hermit. Every afternoon I would attempt to break the previous day's record of how fast I could race home and flip on the television, and more recently, the computer. And there I'd sit with a dual-layer of screens glowing in front of my young eyes for the next few hours. After hearing the welcoming *"You've Got Mail"* of every teenager's mid-nineties staple: AOL (oh who am I kidding? I customized that shit with Thomas Calabro's *"Hey babe"* from some episode of *Melrose Place* as soon as they added that function[3]), I wouldn't even check my buddy list to see how may of my friends from

---

3 Remember how hip AOL used to be? You could customize everything with your favorite movie and television quotes, even the bing-bong of your IM window. It was to the nineties what ring tone and ring-back tones are to today.

school were on. Instead I'd head straight into a chat room—which one didn't really matter in the beginning—and I'd start multiple private conversations in multiple IM windows with multiple strange guys I met in there.

No groaning is necessary: I may have been precocious, but I wasn't completely out of my mind. I never gave my real name or phone number or address; hell, I never even gave my real city or age! Though I always logged in under my primary screen name and therefore, my profile was completely "me"— filled with quotes from my favorite songs and movies at the time— when I chatted in those rooms, I was always an amplified version of myself. I was never a teenage girl sitting at home alone in her New York bedroom; online I could be free to be anyone I wanted, and I took ample advantage of the situation. The character I created, not unlike an avatar in a lot of ways, always had my real voice and personality traits, but those were always placed on someone else's body. I could be who I was but a future version of myself—a better version: DanielleTBD.

When I logged online, I said I was mid-twenties, living in Los Angeles, working in the entertainment industry. Sometimes I was a newlywed, sometimes a recent college graduate, sometimes a young mom. The details didn't often matter, but in doing this in numerous permutations, I was always able to talk about things I cared about with people I thought were mature enough to actually appreciate it. My conversations were never too deeply political or religious, though at times they did dabble, but I was just happy to have an audience at all!

Though the *Culture Of Fear: Tonight At Ten* news media likes to tell stories of Internet-gone-wrong, I never felt a danger in talking to those who were double or triple my age. If a twenty-something wants to talk to a teenager, he may have sinister motives, but a twenty-something is *expected* to want to talk to another twenty-something. And if I was passing...well, that was just the swift kick in the ass my self-esteem needed to skyrocket.

Online I could (and always did) pretend to be someone that I hoped I would one day grow into, and in doing this—in perfecting that person then, years premature— I was able to see what worked and what didn't. I was preparing for the future— sometimes I was a writer, a director, an actress (well, technically I was always an actress!)—and I was "rehearsing" for any future relationships at a safe distance. I didn't see anything wrong with it: AOL chat rooms were the FaceBook for my generation.

My First Boyfriend and I didn't talk about much. He was a musician, so I guess we had the creative thing in common (I had been writing short stories and poetry for years, but I was just starting to branch into screenplays and song lyrics when we met), but something always kept me from holding back. It was exactly as depicted in the episode of *South Park*[4] when the town loses the Internet and everyone migrates west to try to find it...

Shelley Marsh has an online boyfriend with whom she actually comes face to face, but they are dumbstruck in each other's presence. She spends the first twenty minutes of the episode worried that he will forget all about her and go out and get a real girlfriend, and in these mere minutes, she is the most distraught (or displaying human-like emotions at all) that we've ever seen her. While behind the protective wall of the computer screen they are able to talk about their hopes, dreams, desires, likes, and dislikes (presumably), when standing in front of each other, they can only offer weak "*Hi*"s and then stare at the ground as they dig their toes into the dirt. Once they get beckoned away by their parents, it's a joyful: "*See you online; I'll IM you later*!" and Shelley is once again ecstatic that all is well between her and her "boyfriend."

That's kind of how it was for My First Boyfriend and me...though even then, we exchanged few messages online. Often, despite the fact that every afternoon, I ran straight home to hide behind the safety net of phone lines and CPUs, I still found myself ignoring his

4 Season 12, Episode 6: "Overlogging"

"bing bong" message in favor of some of the strangers.' I liked him well enough— and he definitely had the tall, dirty blond, and cute thing going for him— but I was still fixated on a dream and just didn't see myself with him in the long run. And I subscribed to the Shania Twain line of thinking when it came to relationships back then: *"if you [weren't] in it for love; I [was] outta [there]!"*[5]

All right, all right; I know I sound like a real bitch right now, but in reality, it wasn't that I was discriminating towards him: I didn't think *any* high school guy would be serious or mature enough for me. I had these grandiose images of what love and dating and relationships were all about, and quite frankly, *pizza* just wasn't cutting it. There; doesn't that sound better? Le sigh.

Whenever I thought of what dating "should" be, I inevitably reverted to the clichés I had seen on one too many television shows. I wanted slow walks, hand in hand, on the beach (ignoring the forty-minute highway drive that would have been necessary in order to get there from my childhood neighborhood), an evening of dinner and dancing at a club (ignoring the ID that was required for admission *and* the fact that I. Don't. Dance!), and long, late night talks that stretch on into the wee hours but still somehow leave you feeling rejuvenated when you hang up (ignoring my dad's "No phone calls after ten" rule and the fact that I didn't have my own line).

I wanted the kind of "it was destined to be" ease that seemed like it was everywhere I looked—which was solely in the entertainment media. Those were the images being reinforced, regardless of the personalities of the people involved. These were the staples, my "norms," and while I am very aware *now* that it was a limited scope, back then I just assumed it was the natural courtship track.

As a child of the nineties, *Friends* was, of course, my favorite show. You just were not cool if you couldn't show up in homeroom on Friday

5 "(If You're Not in It for Love) I'm Outta Here!" from the 1995 album *"The Woman In Me."*

mornings and quote your favorite moments from the previous night's episode. Like any other night, I jumped into bed at eight o'clock on Thursdays and devoted my full attention to this sitcom gang, but for once I was not alone in the ritual, and there was something almost spiritual about the connection of millions of fans, of all ages and from all across the world, doing the exact same thing at the exact same time. You just don't get that kind of rush with today's DVR programming. But again, that is a diatribe for a later time.

Just like how years prior *Saved by the Bell* gave me a taste of what I hoped high school would be, *Friends* offered me glimpses into the until-then-unknown "twenty-something" mystery. As an only child, I had no frame of reference from an older brother or sister, so Ross, Chandler, Joey, Rachel, Monica, and Phoebe were my tour guides.

Even as a kid (the show debuted in 1994 when I was only ten), it was clear to me the arc they were attempting to take for Ross and Rachel. From moment one (in "The One Where It All Began" or "The One Where Monica Gets A Roommate"), they set it up so that they were *"lobsters,"* as Phoebe, in her flakey wisdom, tried to explain, or "soul mates" (at least by television's standards) to everyone else.

Ross sits in the coffee house, depressed over his wife leaving him for another woman and woefully exclaims that he "just wants to be married again" when Rachel, clad in a damp wedding dress, bursts through the doors in the most on-the-nose answer to his prayers. Ross takes one look at her and knows immediately: she was, after all, the girl for whom he had longed since the ninth grade.

I never particularly liked Ross—for Rachel or in general. He was always too whiny, too wimpy, too...*cartoonish* to be taken seriously as a man or a love interest in my discriminating and not-so-humble opinion. And though Rachel said his hair was always more "crunchy" than it was greasy, just looking at the top of his head always made me want to open a fire hydrant on him. Still, he was a *huge* romantic, and his gestures, though occasionally ill timed, always came from the heart, sweetening and endearing himself to me. When he dressed up as a sailor and quite literally swept Rachel off her feet and whisked her out of the coffeehouse; when his birthday gift to her was something thoughtful and meaningful and about which only he would know; when he canceled a television appearance to attend to her injuries even though they weren't even together; or when he described their picture-perfect future, despite it freaking her out at the time, even the iciest child's heart melted just a teeny bit. Ahem.

I've always been much more about the ends than the means, meaning I don't care so much about the journey but just where it would lead me. Ross and Rachel, and the audience in turn, could tell they loved each other just by simply looking at each other. Sure there was tons of back and forth over the years to create the will-they-won't-they drama that kept everybody watching, but Chandler said it best when he quite literally cried: *"I just don't see why those two can't work things out!"* It was always inevitable that they would end the show in each other's arms; it just hadn't been written *how* they'd get to that point yet.

It was also just as inevitable that Monica and Chandler would end up together—though the hints flew pretty under the radar for a while, as the audience was mostly distracted with Ross and Rachel's back and forth. Still, it quite obviously started as far back as the first Thanksgiving episode,[6] when they were spying on Ugly Naked Guy "having Thanksgiving dinner with Ugly Naked gal" through Monica and Rachel's living room window. Phoebe turned to the group and said it was "nice that he [had] someone:" Chandler and Monica looked at each other knowingly, and though it was subtle, it was the first seed that something far greater was to come.

At the end of the first season in "The One With The Birth," though, those seeds began to get more strategically planted when Monica started to fear she would never get married and have a family of

6 Season 1, Episode 9: "The One Where Underdog Gets Away"

her own, and Chandler offered to marry her if neither of them were settled down by the time they were thirty. At the time it aired, it seemed like just a nice gesture for a friend to make in order to attempt to console her, but the underlying tones were all there, and in a very *Sixth Sense* sort of way, all came together when you went back and viewed the episode later—perhaps even after the series finale— knowing now what you didn't then.

Once Monica and Chandler finally did get together, the writers took us even further back as extra clarification to explain that they were always meant to be—from Monica thinking Chandler was cute and hanging on his every word (like "You should be a chef") when she first met him in "The One With All The Thanksgivings" to them still hooking up in "The One That Could Have Been" even though she was still Fat Monica. There was no alternative ending for them: they were always supposed to become "The Bings." Some days, I still hope to see that spin-off being announced at the Upfronts.

When I looked at My First Boyfriend, though, all I saw was a sort-of hopefulness. He was soft-spoken and mild-mannered and never pushed me when I said I had to sign offline but then only logged out of our particular IM conversation. I'm sure I was unconsciously testing him with those afternoons—to see if he'd keep at me, keep *pursuing* me the way I saw on all of those shows. It wasn't enough, I knew, just to declare yourself in a relationship with someone...but I also knew enough to know that if the connection wasn't there immediately, you couldn't force it. Ross once told Rachel to *"start looking"* at him in that romantic way, though she had never seen him as anything more than a friend before, and I scoffed. There are reasons, I knew even back then, that a guy is a platonic friend and nothing more. If you didn't look at him "that way" when you first met him, you wouldn't change your mind. It might work for Ross and Rachel, a fake couple in a fictional version of New York, but out on the real city streets, I felt like I needed more. I needed all I had been seeing about it being destiny, and I wasn't going to settle for anything less than what I had been building up in my mind for so many years.

So I decided I didn't want to waste my time trying to force something into that mold if it wasn't a natural fit.

Looking back now, I can honestly say that if I hadn't been so blinded by the *stars in my eyes*[7], so to speak, maybe we could have gone the distance (at least in the short term world that is high school). I never really got to know him in those few months we were "together" because I was so preoccupied with my own preconceived assumptions that I never really stopped to look at him and see if something greater *was* possible.

In fact when we finally broke up (over IM, no less!), it was because Christmas was coming up, and I flat out told him I didn't think I knew him well enough to know what he'd want as a holiday gift. I took that as a sign that we weren't meant to be, and he didn't disagree. Neither of us pointed out that if I felt that way, maybe we just needed to spend more time together to *get* to know each other, even though I knew at least *I* was definitely thinking it.

Years later, when we were seniors, I started to see him again in that light like when we were newbs. He had a new girlfriend by then, though, and we had already spent the majority of the past four years exchanging nothing more than simple, occasional pleasantries in class or SING rehearsal. When I realized the initial attraction was back, I attempted to infiltrate his world but got little past asking him what he thought of the latest Eminem single. I guess I still felt pretty awkward about how I had left things...just because I was able to fool virtual strangers into believing I was already a grown-up, I was still young enough to actually use terms like "grown-up," and none of that made me as mature as I liked to think I was.

I guess My First Boyfriend just never really stood a chance then, and in reality, it had absolutely nothing to do with him. I may not have been a passive television viewer, but I was certainly passive when it came to my own life, preferring instead to live vicariously

7 The title of my debut, self-published novel, available now at amazon.com!

through on-screen examples and relationships than going out and experiencing anything for myself. It was safer that way. Even my online relationships were safer because those guys couldn't catch me if they were chasing someone who didn't exist, but My First Boyfriend was standing right in front of me, and for all of my talk, I wasn't truly ready to be caught.

THE SOUNDTRACK TO MY LIFE...

By the time I was in high school I was pretty much just counting down the days until my eighteenth birthday (no *"that's what he said"* jokes, please) when I could legally move out of my parents' apartment and three-thousand miles west across the country to never return. You know what they— or at least *Gilmore Girls*— say about California: "You don't come back from [there]; it changes you!"[8] For me, California seemed like the place that I could finally be myself. So I set a plan in motion to set up camp on the sands of Santa Monica, just north enough of the Paradise Cove with which I fell in love during a semi-guided tour of a fictional version of Redondo by the *California Dreams* gang, that I could rollerblade down there on weekends for a shake and a song.

In 1992, NBC announced the expansion of its Saturday morning "kid-friendly" programming while simultaneously dropping its cartoon line-up and instead boasting a companion piece to the already popular *Saved by the Bell,* which was sadly on its last legs and making way for a new freshmen class that could never quite capture the shine of the original. Also set in a fictitious Southern California high school— though very little time was actually spent around lockers and books, proving what I had already assumed to be true: the most fun things happened *outside* of the classroom— *California Dreams* took off where *SBTB* only dabbled: in the creative and entrepreneurial talents of its lead characters.

8 Season 4, Episode 4: "Chicken or Beef?"

Sure, Zack Morris was always looking for new get-rich-quick-schemes, but his were flashes in the pan. He'd try a radio station one episode and run track in the next; his job was to introduce the kids of the nineties to a variety of things that could be cool. The *Dreams* gang, on the other hand, had their one niche, and they stuck with it. They showed kids of the nineties that it could be cool to find what you love at an early age and work hard to be really, really good at it.

The Dreams managed to find an outlet that worked to not only bring them together as a group (whereas Zack's exploits usually had the rest of his buddies mad at him for a hot minute before *"Aw shucks"*-ing and playfully punching him on the arm) but also to show *me* that unsigned musicians were sometimes worth taking a second look.

To this day the "Zack Attack" episode of *SBTB* is my favorite of the series, hands down, if only because of the somewhat badly lip-synced original songs. *California Dreams*, though, featured a "performance" in every episode, and these were teens who were playing outside of the comfort of their own garage and at the real (and moderately trafficked!) arena of a local restaurant. They showed no reservations; they didn't worry about other kids calling "musical poetry" uncool; and they were always in it for the fun— despite cousin Sly's best efforts to get them paid gigs. That was the kind of laidback fun that I wanted to be around!

The Dreams were comfortable with themselves and their passions, and they were uninhibited about sharing them with the world. That was something I strove to match. Problem was: I had no musical talent whatsoever— though after tireless afternoons of rewinding my *The Little Mermaid* soundtrack cassette to "Part of your World" over and over, I was pretty convinced I nailed *those* vocals! My personal collection consisted of all fancily-coiffed and packaged artists like NKOTB, BSB,[9] Madonna, and Mariah Carey. I wanted a lifestyle I didn't

9 That's New Kids on the Block and The Backstreet Boys, respectively, for those of you pretending to be too cool too remember the phenomena!

think I'd be able to truly adopt unless I brought someone else in with me—someone else who had the true musical ear that I lacked.

My Second Boyfriend (no trademark is necessary here; there is something far less marketable, let alone magical, about sloppy seconds) was in the school band. For someone who admittedly has a pretty limited and specific library of personal music interest and knowledge *("to answer your earlier question, we're straight-up hardcore gangsta rap"[10])*, the irony of how many musicians (no matter how small potatoes) with whom I have hooked up is most certainly not lost on me. It wasn't exactly The Dreams—My Second Boyfriend played the unsexy instrument of the flute—but it would do.

Like me, My Second Boyfriend scribbled furiously in class. And again like me, his notes were all lines from original pieces on which he said he was writing. He was putting together a band, in which he could *shred* guitar. He sometimes doodled musical notes in the margins of his notebooks, too— but since I couldn't actually read music, I perhaps somewhat naively assumed they were nothing more than a bored kid's drawings, the way I sketched eyes or hearts with arrows piercing them on my own sheets of loose leaf. For all I know, though, he could have been composing hit melodies in second and third period. Up until a few years ago when MTV stopped playing music, I used to look for him to pop up in the new countdowns. He certainly seemed to have the potential for that—or at least, I really wanted him to.

Though My Second Boyfriend's Upper West Side—and Upper Middle Class—Wasp-y last name begged to differ, whenever I looked at his shaggy, sandy brown hair and lightly freckled face, I saw a west coast bohemian—one who belonged on the boardwalk of Venice Beach, strumming the same guitar in the same carefree

10 Friends' Season 8, Episode 10: "The One With Monica's Boots." Joey tries to befriend his little sister's boyfriend who got her pregnant and asks what kind of music he and his band, Numb Nuts, perform.

manner. In fact, My Second Boyfriend first caught my eye when he slid into the desk opposite me in our semi-circle set-up of English class because he looked like a lighter-haired Brent Gore, the lead singer in the fictitious *California Dreams* band. I even started humming the theme song in the halls on my way to that class for a full two weeks before he finally came up to me to ask if I'd want to see a movie sometime. As a non-threatening and somewhat shy guitarist, My Second Boyfriend was one part Matt Garrison and one part Mark Winkle, and just like the easy success of Paradise Cove's resident entertainment, our relationship felt slightly unreal.

When My Second Boyfriend and I went to the movies, we didn't sit in the back row and start kissing when the previews came up, as was stereotypical and somewhat expected in my neighborhood. He didn't even snake his arm around the back of my chair and gently nudge my head to rest on his shoulder, as I told my friends had happened. My Second Boyfriend was the perfect gentleman. In fact, he was a little *too Pleasantville*-inspired. Call me old-fashioned or call me a stereotypical girl—and of both I admit I am guilty—but I like the guy to make the first move, and My Second Boyfriend never tried to go in for anything more than a simple peck on the corner of my mouth, as if he had been aiming for my cheek but slipped. If I didn't know better, I would have sworn, he, too, was playing by the "this is how they did it on NBC Saturday mornings" playbook of dating...which was weird because, for as much as I was looking for a guy who shared my same love of television (and interest in *specific* shows), most straight guys didn't get my references!

And I know, I know; I was the one that wanted such traditional behavior, and yet there I was, all of fifteen and already jaded enough to find it corny.

For all of My Second Boyfriend's guitar toting and talk of having me give him feedback, though, he never actually organized a band, let alone practices. My Second Boyfriend was not a burnout by any means, but he *did* hang out on The Wall (a quite literal concrete slab just in front of the tennis courts next to my school where most kids went when they needed to meet their dealer). His guitar case would be slung over his shoulder, but it seemed increasingly rare that he actually played the...axe? Is that the right term? To this day, I'm still a bit of a musical lame duck. More and more, though, I began to find the idea or image of him as a boyfriend much more interesting than the actual guy who was standing in front of me.

SURF DUDE WITHOUT ATTITUDE...

Jake Sommers rode into the *California Dreams* gang—and even if you didn't know the show, you undoubtedly knew the kind of guy: maybe he moved into town late in life or changed districts abruptly in the middle of your high school career or just got introduced through mutual friends at a park or party or teen club— always slightly mysterious and seemingly with a bit of an edge. Jake, in particular, sported an earring, a motorcycle jacket, and a *wicked* talent. But perhaps most importantly, he managed to pique a teen girl's interest without completing putting off the parents (just from where do you think the Jonas Brothers learned??). Unfortunately for the other guys in The Dreams, Jake completely stole the spotlight. And similarly (and unfortunately) for My Second Boyfriend, the summer of 2000 an athlete nicknamed (by me now, not then...as if that makes it any better!) Tan Man rode—err, *swam* into my life and stole *my* attention.

Blame it on the fast-paced editing of MTV (everyone else during that time did, even though I didn't even *have* MTV in my household), but my attention span for television was short, and my attention span for guys was even shorter. I would become *obsessed* with one (show or guy, take your pick!) for months on end, wanting to watch and talk about nothing but that, but if I found it wasn't giving me what I really wanted in return, I was quite fickle—a young girl scorned, if you will— and I would drop it quickly. I was always looking for the next (better) thing, dutifully believing that because each new season enthralled me with a new show, the same would be true when it came to guys.

Or maybe the allure of being with a guy in a band really *isn't* for everyone. It is stereotypical for girls to swoon and throw their bras onstage for any guy with an instrument in his hand, but it proved to be more of a novelty for me than something that I really wanted. After all, I knew nothing of that world, so I couldn't relate, and sooner or later I just knew we'd inevitably drift apart due to "creative differences."

So when I decided I wanted to move on sooner rather than later, I justified the premature and somewhat unfound dumping as none of the above but instead simply going for what I *really* wanted. And what I *really* wanted, I realized, was that kind of laid-back, go with the flow, sit on the sand all day and stare at the sea, musician *attitude*... but I didn't actually need the gear to go with it.

When I was sixteen, I worked as a junior counselor at a day camp in my neighborhood. It was a place I had been going to for six weeks every summer since I was five, and it was a place I had come to loathe. I'd dream instead of renting an empty cabin by a lake and having my own summer time adventure with Jonathan Jackson, Marnette (then Marnie) Patterson, and Andrew Keegan.

Being that mine was a sports camp, I didn't have much use for it, after all, nor did I desire to be one of the counselors who told their campers their *"parents [were] paying good money for them to be there, so you better not just sit on your butt in the grass all day!"* I had certainly heard that one too many times directed at me over the years, and no one seemed to like the: *"If my parents are paying you, don't you think you should let me do whatever I want?"* standard response I gave.

I sat in the wide oak hall of the main administrative building (during the non-humid months of the year, the camp's ground were actually a prestigious private school) awaiting my interview with the headmaster, whose job it would be to see if I was deemed "fit" enough to watch over twenty-something spoiled rich kids pawned off by their own parents who didn't want to bother attempting to keep them entertained as the temperature climbed. I admit I thought of quite of a few ways I could "throw" the meeting…and not in my favor. I was an only child, and I figured I could use that lack of experience being around other, younger kids to my advantage.

As I waited for the headmaster to beckon me into the office, some guy in basketball shorts and sneakers with the laces tucked lazily behind the tongue and into the sides slid past my chair and into the one across from me. I was far too engrossed with trying to beat my high-score at Snake on the now-archaic green analog screen of my old Nokia cell phone to notice, let alone acknowledge, that someone else was in my presence. It was only when my name was finally called and I stood to cross his path that I casually threw a glance his way, and my heart skipped a beat.

Tan Man, a legend among all teen girls within a twenty-block radius, didn't need a guitar as a gimmick (which I was now convinced was the only reason My Second Boyfriend had one at all) to get girls interested in him. I marveled at how this boy could be only a year older than my own guy friends and yet tower over them— and quite literally, too— to seem like he was at least in college.

With his long, lean swimmer's build, I could practically see his abs through his white wife-beater tank, and that alone set him apart: I didn't know abs existed outside of my television! And even there, I assumed some sort of make-up was involved to make them appear more pronounced than they really were.

His face was pleasantly acne-free, and when he smiled, as he did at me then, his perfect line of teeth were off-set nicely by the rich tan already set deeply into his skin, despite summer still not quite yet on our horizon. He looked like a bronze statue, one that was only missing a surfboard tucked under his arm. His hair was cropped short, highlighted, and home to some product: he was a metrosexual before the term was coined. He was obviously confident and comfortable with himself, and that made him sexier than any of the rest of it.

I offered a meek smile in return and headed in to face what I had assumed would be my doom with a renewed vigor. Needless to say,

I was now going to do everything I could to ensure I *did* get the gig. If it meant working alongside this guy, those six weeks would no longer be dreaded but gloriously savored.

As I sat down on the cold, oversized leather chair inside the headmaster's office, I found myself quite chatty with the man who would become my boss. I suddenly wanted—no, I *needed*—him to want me for this job. In the three seconds it took for me to cross the threshold, I had experienced an epiphany: I suddenly wanted—no I *needed*—to work at the camp this summer. Seeing Tan Man wait for face-time with this guy meant he, too, had just applied for a summer job there, and being that his father was the local pediatrician, there was no way he would be denied. The camp, like the prep school the grounds housed during the other nine months of the year, was built on prestige and donations, and to have a local celebrity of sorts in its mix was a must. Nepotism ran rampant, even on the streets of Brooklyn, three thousand miles away from Hollywood.

I saw this as my shot to finally get a little taste of what those *Dreams* kids had been singing about: I was already convinced I belonged in California because of how much I loved the surf, sand, and sea, and though I didn't truly know any of it to be a fact, everything about Tan Man's appearance said he agreed. In a city of Guidos with thick gold chains and hair gelled up into sharp spikes, Tan Man was a cool breath of ocean air.

I walked out of the office with an extra pep in my step that was caused simply by the mere two-seconds I had stared at Tan Man; it has always been the littlest things that get me excited and send me on a "high," so to speak. Tan Man was still sitting where I had left him, proving that he would make a very reliable and conscientious boyfriend, and this time I surprised myself by actually saying hello.

I don't know from where it came; it was like the high was turning me into someone else entirely—someone completely uninhibited. It was strange, yet intriguing, and I wanted to see what would happen next.

"You're Tan Man,[11] right?" I asked, plopping back down on the original chair but this time with my cell phone tucked safely into the back pocket of my jeans.

He nodded and asked me how I knew.

"Oh, your dad's my doctor," I shrugged like an idiot.

The look on his face sobered me up pretty quickly; it was the look of a guy who had been hearing the same thing every day of his life, and to say the least, he seemed to be sick of it. But the way I saw it, it could have been worse; his dad was the local pediatrician, not gynecologist!

Despite my initial misstep, we spent the next few minutes talking before he said he had to go. I had been planning to walk home myself after the interview— and maybe stop to get an Italian ice along the way. He would fit nicely into those plans: suddenly the chore of trekking half a mile to my tiny apartment would be replaced by a romantic sunset stroll. The only problem was that I couldn't work up the nerve to ask him to join me. Instead, in what I can only describe as a moment of "the God I wasn't entirely sure existed until that moment throwing me a bone for once in my young life," he asked me if I wanted a ride. And for once, I somehow managed not to put my foot in my mouth and f*ck up the invitation.

Unfortunately, I *was* dumb enough to tell all my friends about it the next day via IM after IM. In doing so, I built it up so much in my mind that I actually started to believe it could be the start of something, even though I could hear the dorky chorus of "Summer Lovin" in my head as I typed.

When orientation arrived—I got that junior counselor position, and Tan Man was hired as a lifeguard—weeks had gone by without

---

11 Don't worry; I used his *real* name. His full name, but his real name nonetheless.

us talking, though we had exchanged screen names that afternoon, and I found myself logging on and off of AOL all day, waiting for a moment when he would be on, too, and then hoping he would start a conversation. He never did. I guess I could have, but I never did, either. Instead, I chose to just imagine possibilities: I created a whole arc in my head about spending my free periods— when my campers were in art class or tennis lessons or the dance studio— sitting next to him at the pool, our legs dangling in the cold water, laughing, holding hands, and growing closer. We would stay together through the school year, but we would never go to each other's respective dances, as I found them tacky, and I *just knew* he agreed.

I spied Tan Man (because, let's face it, even as I was chatting with friends, I was glancing over their shoulders, scanning the crowd looking for him) hanging out on the steps of the courtyard during the orientation, talking with some guys I knew from years past when the camp groups were co-ed. I just sort of smiled and nodded at him. It was a gesture so miniscule that he probably didn't even notice I was directing it at him, despite the pair of glitter-dusted denim Capri pants that I picked out specially to catch his eye during this occasion. I made sure to nudge my friends closer and closer to his group throughout the evening, though, talking louder and louder with the hope that he would overhear something particularly witty and head over, throwing his arm around my shoulders and asking to be introduced to everyone.

As the night wore on, I grew more and more frustrated— and equally as passive aggressive, I feel I would be remiss if I didn't note, because *yes*, I was aware of it, but I wasn't proud of it.

I babbled about anything I knew we had talked about on that first evening to try to catch his eye— or ear, as it were. I laughed loudly about something that happened on *The Simpsons*, a show I only started watching in the last few weeks because he snarkily quoted it in passing. I announced to the courtyard in general that I was hoping at least one or two of the kids in my group wouldn't know how to swim so I could offer private lessons on the side for some extra cash because I wanted him to know that despite what he may hear about my spastic athletics from years past, swimming was the one thing at which I was quite natural, and dare I say it, *graceful,* just like him. I even allowed two of my friends to pull me into a semi-circle and dance (or sway, as it were, trying to pretend I was too distracted by my Diet Coke to really move too much) to the Top 40 hits blaring out of an old boom box. Desperate really was spelled D-a-n-i-e-l-l-e that evening!

It wasn't until I practically screamed to my best friend how I was so happy I actually passed my chemistry final exam, as it was a subject I was sure we had bonded over not understanding, that I stepped outside of myself and actually *witnessed* the desperation, though.

I floated above myself momentarily, as said best friend "Uh-huhed" at me and rolled her eyes before slipping into the crowd to find one of less self-involved (at least at this moment) mutual friends. I could have used that opportunity to saunter up to Tan Man. I could have, and I probably should have, but that wouldn't have been my style. Instead I stomped up the steps and through the hall to the front circle to make a fake phone call.

Side note: when I was in junior high, I had a friend who said that the best defense if you think someone is following you when you're walking home alone late at night would be to start talking to the trees and streetlamps and trashcans because then your would-be attacker would think you're crazier than he is and let you go on your merry way. But I thought whipping out a cell phone, for those of us who were spoiled enough to have them at that age, and pretending to dial someone up, would work just as well. Such a thing also worked when you were stuck at the mall, waiting for a friend to finish in a dressing room and you ran into someone else from school that you're sort-of friends with but didn't invite on this shopping trip. For safety or simply to alleviate a potentially awkward situation, I didn't care; it *worked*! And I still think I'm due some sort of residuals on that "Fake-A-Call" iPhone App because of it!

Anyway, I stayed out in the front circle for what was probably the better part of half an hour, pretending I was talking to some older friend, helping *her* with a problem, hoping my voice was loud enough to carry to the back so he could hear just how mature I was. At least I remembered to turn my ringer off, though, because although I'm sure my voice was drowned out by the music and laughter, something tells me that had my phone rang when I was supposedly already on a call, *everyone* would have heard, and I would have been busted. That's just my luck.

I spent the summer of 2000 sitting out by the pool during my free periods, like I had planned. I usually brought a book or my cell phone and kept myself just busy enough that if he didn't make an effort to talk to me, I could look like I wasn't just sitting out there waiting for him to come over.

A few of the girls in the group I was responsible for that summer developed crushes on Tan Man, too (well-deserved ones, I might add!). One day when I brought my camera to camp, they stood on the balcony with it for almost half an hour, whispering and giggling and calling his name so he would look up from the pool in their general direction so they could snap a photograph.

Okay confession time: *of course* I still have the one shot they managed to take of him looking directly into the lens and grinning wildly. I have tucked it into a "memory box" of things from my childhood, sandwiched between a Mary-Kate & Ashley Olsen "Brother 4 Sale" CD and my favorite Polly Pocket. I think of it—and him—occasionally and wonder whatever happened to him. I may never know, as he doesn't appear to have a Facebook page because *believe* me; I've checked!

Just a few months ago, though, I was walking through the parking lot to a popular movie theater and restaurant complex in

Los Angeles, and I passed a car with the vanity plate TANMAN1. My heart momentarily skipped a beat, and sixteen year-old me fluttered back just briefly enough to glimpse us bumping into each other all these years later and starting something now, when we—or at least *I* was actually mature enough to be ready. But then I just shook it off, snapped a photo of the license plate for that memory box, and kept walking on to my own car. I try not to let my imagination wander *too* far these days, and I consider that progress!

I also try not to dwell on the fact that back then two nine year-olds had shared the same kind of relationship with him that I did!

Tan Man and I exchanged small pleasantries over the six-week course of camp, but we never really interacted on a deeper level. Tan Man wasn't exactly clawing through the chain-link fence around the pool to get to me, and I admit I was a bit put-off by, or at least nervous about, the rumors that he and one of the wealthier (and bitchier!) counselors had dated throughout the school year but broke up when she got suspended for having drugs in her locker. I was pretty vanilla, as a life reared by "There's no hope with dope" Very Special sitcom episodes would beget. I didn't know for sure that he was mixed up in any of that, but a part of me was scared to find out…and risk ruining the "perfect" image of him I had created in my own mind.

Also I knew it could never work out between us because I was leaving for California just two short summers from then. And I, in my finite childhood "wisdom," just couldn't see the point in starting something so great if I knew I wouldn't be able to finish it.

When Jenny went off to Italy for a semester on *California Dreams,* she and Jake had to break up. If they couldn't make a long-distance thing work, I didn't have much hope for me doing so, either…I knew Jenny and Jake were fictional characters, but I chose to follow their example instead of actually risk getting hurt by trying to learn from one of my own. I was the worst kind of hypocrite, and I self-sabotaged in the worst possible way— to the point where I wasn't even willing to *try.*

Or maybe I simply got scared. Though *California Dreams* taught me the "bad boy" often had a heart of gold underneath his leather jacket, I really had no worldly experience to tell me if that was true. And Lord knows if it wasn't, I had no worldly experience to be able to change him, either!

I'M A CHILD; I'M A MOTHER...I'M NOTHING IN BETWEEN...

Desperate as I may have been at times (read: that one year after I turned twelve when I was still sorting out what I wanted out of this life) to believe in the "can't eat, can't sleep, reach for the stars, over the fence world series kind of love,"[12] growing up in New York made me too jaded to feel like I could rely on actually finding it. After all, the sarcastic, slightly frumpy brunette best friend in the movies never ends up getting the guy. So instead, I very quickly turned my attention toward love of a different kind: maternal. It sounds anti-feminist now, but for every time as I was told I was "so ambitious and driven" as a child, I could count three more when I thought to myself that all I wanted to do in my life was be a stay-at-home mom.

I played house as a kid—mostly in my Fisher Price kitchen set—but standing at the short counter with the flimsy plastic plates and fake cupcakes, I often felt more like a waitress or even a line cook than a mother. In truth, just like how Michelle on *Full House* once wanted to be Uncle Joey while playing house with her own BFF because she didn't have a mommy (hers died when she was just an infant, and so the concept of three men and three little ladies—one of which was still a baby—was born), my own mother was absent so much I might have forgotten what she looked like— if I didn't already have her nose!

My mother awoke every morning at four a.m. in order to get to work before the sun did, and when she arrived back at our apartment

12 *It Takes Two*; Warner Brothers; 1995.

around dinnertime, it was mostly to ask if I had any tests for which I should be studying. I have been told that in the early years, I would wait in the living room for the sound of the key in the front door and then crawl—and later, teeter unsteadily upright on two chubby little toddler legs—toward the sound so that she could scoop me up in a hug when she came home. I don't remember this, and there is no photographic evidence to prove truth. However, our family Golden Retriever used to bound over to the door the second she heard the key turning in the lock, and chances are she had to learn that *some*where...

As an only child, I was left on my own to play single mother, with my children a hodgepodge collection of stuffed dogs, bears, and American Girl dolls. I relished the idea of having a diverse family, but my imagination must not have been as vast as I always assumed it to be because I quickly found I preferred instead to find some real life characters and incorporate them into my fantasy world. My children of choice, therefore, were those two adorable little tow-headed girls behind Michelle that I found on my favorite TGIF program: *Full House*.

Though in actuality Ashley and Mary-Kate Olsen were only two years younger than me, watching their toothless precociousness play out in witty one-liners or simple eye-rolls on screen made me feel a sense of pride. I didn't want to be in their shoes, experiencing all of the cool things and people (hel-*lo*, Uncle Jesse!), but I certainly wanted to be a *part* of that world. No, I didn't want to *be* them; I wanted to be *better* than them!

I created a character for myself to be then—based on the twins' own mother about whom I knew a little from fan 'zines. Yes, I'm serious. And since I spent almost eight hours a day in school, the classroom was something I felt I knew pretty well, so it only seemed natural for me to expand the character into not just a mother but also a teacher, which, when you really think about it, is usually pretty much synonymous anyway. I didn't so much as play house as I did school, and that was only because it was my only real reference of authority.

I didn't know enough about the television industry then as a six or seven year old to know that on-set school did not resemble my own, where we sat in desk-clusters of four, with painted six-pack containers as our "racks" to hold pencils, markers, and Elmer's glue. I certainly knew something about favoritism, though, and I was definitely guilty of falling prey to it in my make-believe classroom.

In my own classroom, we had one of those cardboard charts on the wall that marked our progress. We got stickers for every test on which we got 100%, and at the end of the quarter, whoever had the most stickers would get a prize—something like an extra five points on the next test or a free item at book sale time. Since I was in an accelerated class (I refuse to call us "gifted," for fear Kathy Griffin will mock me mercilessly—and she'd be right to), we were all pitted against each other in a direct competition to be the best of the best, the cream of the crop, the "heirs to the throne," so to speak. And it didn't always seem like it was really about us, either: whoever's mother or father was "Room Parent" undoubtedly received special privileges from the teachers, who were probably just so grateful at the extra help they would have given the child solid E (for Excellent) s on his or her report card regardless of whether or not even a single scrap of loose leaf assignment was ever turned in again.

But that year, in the first grade, I didn't know all of this just yet. All I knew was that I was finally on a streak—one that was uniquely mine: I was the only child in my crowded public school class to get 100% on every spelling test. It was my claim to fame— my "thing"— and though it certainly wasn't anything I could put on a college application— especially considering I later went to high school with the National Spelling Bee Champion of 1997— it was still what set me apart from the other children and marked me as special at the time.

I remember one particular afternoon when I held my spelling homework tight to my chest, staring at the lump of my father sprawled on the couch in front of me. I stood motionlessly, even though a cold draft blew through the frosted living room window, causing my hair to dance around my shoulders, and sighed and took a step forward.

My father's eyelids fluttered, even though they appeared crusted shut. His mouth hung open. The television remote rose up and down on his chest in tune with his breathing. His white undershirt was stained yellow under the arms. His snoring seemed to echo in my ears as I stepped forward, leaning over him. Now, I am not trying to James Frey it up here, but you have to understand that even at such a young age, I saw things as if I was looking through a camera lens at all times. Everything was heightened, intensified, and cinematic—not unlike how Kevin sees the basement furnace as a monster in the beginning of *Home Alone*. Childhood imaginations often create better stories than anything any director could.

Stoically, I picked up the television remote and pressed the big red button in the top corner. The news anchor stopped droning on in mid-sentence. I hadn't even heard the man's voice over the snores anyway. I shook my father's shoulder, calling his name, and his arm flopped over the side of the couch. He grunted but didn't wake up right away. When he finally did, I just thrust the sheet of loose-leaf at him, and he took it, squinting. His eyes barely glanced over the words before he thrust it back, saying it was good and that I should just leave him alone and let him sleep.

That Friday my class took our weekly spelling test, and in the afternoon, when she was handing them back, she patted my shoulder as the paper fluttered down onto my desk. I turned it around and around but still the number remained the same: 90%. There was a big red X next to number four. I crumpled the paper and shoved it into the back of my desk, right alongside the old wads of gum the custodians hadn't been able to scrape off over the summer before the new students took the classroom. Whoever sat next to me at that point probably asked how I did, but I'm sure I didn't admit the mistake I made; I probably lied and said my usual one hundred. Pride consumed me even then.

After the bell rang, I held the balled-up paper in my right hand, clenching a fist with the left, and stepped up to my teacher's desk, tossing the ball on the surface. I was a brazen little bitch! I asked—no let's be real here, I *demanded*— to take the test over. My teacher, who was in her first year at the school, let alone the profession, thought I was nuts, to put it nicely. With only one question wrong, I had done very well, but not well enough for me. The following year I would keep up this trend by occasionally erasing some wrong answers and filling in the right ones after science and social studies tests were handed back, saying my teacher must have graded them wrong. I would claw my way to the top at any cost!

I explained to my ingénue of a teacher in as calm and probably condescending a voice as I could muster that my father had been checking my homework all week, and I reminded her that she, too, had skimmed the pages when it came time to give credit for the assignments. I had been spelling the word wrong all week, and no one had noticed or said anything to me to help me correct it.

To this day, I have no idea what that word was, by the way, but I remember feeling outraged and as if I had been unjustly targeted. My father and my teacher couldn't possibly have just been distracted or neglectful; they were malicious in their attempt to keep me from another sticker on the chart!

Somehow in my finite six-year-old wisdom, I convinced my teacher (or she placated me…*semantics*!) to let me stay after school for a second chance. I gave "do it yourself" a new definition; while my friends had their parents covering their asses and doing assignments for them, I was quite literally taking charge of my own education. So I guess it only seemed a logical step to try to take charge of others'… even if it was just pretend.

I selected a wide variety of my dolls to be my students— size and material were never an issue, as I did not discriminate in my classroom— and gave them all names and "roles," so to speak.

There was Eric, played by a trench coat wearing teddy bear, perhaps ironically identical to the one Stephanie dragged around on *Full House*, who was the most popular boy in the class and the one on whom all of the girls had crushes; there was Billy, the star baseball player, played by my tuxedo sporting Mickey Mouse; there were Amy and Chelsea, each played by a different "Babysitter's Club" doll and who were the other two cool kids to round up the foursome; and then of course there was Dylan, who was the class troublemaker and the only less-than-stellar student, who quite frankly made the whole game ten times more fun than any of the other dull, goody-goodies!

I had two of my most special and newest dolls set aside for my star pupils, Ashley and Mary-Kate, too: the dolls were what I considered at the time to be fraternal, just like the real life twins. One was a baby doll with no hair, and the other was a toddler with a full head of curly blonde locks, but the faces were identical, each with little red hearts on their cheeks that you could make show up by swiping them clean with a warm washcloth. They were Magic Nursery Baby dolls, and though I'm sure those hearts had some other significance or purpose at the time, I can't for the life of me now remember what it may have been. I'm sure you can Google it or find a gently used one on eBay.

I originally wanted just the toddler doll. I didn't figure I could get my mother to buy me *two* for Christmas, considering they weren't like Barbies, and each one didn't come with its own different outfit or occupation, so I planned to use the one to play both Ashley and Mary-Kate, just like how they played one character on their show. When Ashley was in her chair at school, Mary-Kate could be off in the bathroom…or on-set, and vice versa. I thought my plan was pretty genius, and I wrote to Santa that year asking for a brand new Nursery Baby doll.

Since Santa is supposed to be all-knowing— he knew when I was asleep, awake, good, and bad, for chrissakes!— I didn't think I had to specify that I wanted the toddler with the pretty, pretty hair of golden blonde curls that I envied just the teeniest, tiniest little bit.

He should have been omnipotent enough to just *know* I wanted it just like how if I ran into him on the street, I expected him to know my name. We're all one of Santa's children, after all![13]

But that Christmas morning, the Homer-Simpson-bald (read: one curly strand of hair protruding from the middle of the head) baby stared back at me through a thin plastic window on the box instead. I tried to hide my disappointment, but I was never a good actress, even though I had had the lead in that year's holiday play. When my mother asked what was wrong, I pointed out that Santa must not be as inherently brilliant as we all thought because he had taken the brand name of the doll "Magic Nursery Baby" to be the description. My mother replied with: "Santa can make mistakes, too," but it was too late. He made one small slip up, but it was enough for me to stop believing in him and his whole magic hoop-la.

My mother later braved the post-holiday return madness at Toys R Us to get me the "right" doll, but I kept the baby, too, and I used them as representations of the creative, intelligent, talented, and hardworking little girls I hoped to someday have for real. In a way, I was envious of them too: things seemed to come so easily to the Olsen twins. They literally fell into acting at the age of nine months when their mother took them on a casting call on a whim, and they were an immediate success. Adults everywhere cooed at how adorable they were, and little girls everywhere copied their mannerisms and catch phrases. I guess I fell somewhere in the middle.

When I was in fifth grade, I took on the lunchtime job of "table monitor" for the current first grade class that was being taught by my own ex-first grade teacher. Though I wasn't conducting any official school business, day in and day out I helped serve lunches, kept the kids seated and relatively quiet in the lunchroom, and then oversaw and reinforced the rules of playground games. I

---

13 In a way, I kind of thought "Santa" was just a substitute term to introduce kids to the idea of "God;" he did watch over the world's children and answer their prayers and all. And we had to be just as good to get presents as we did to go to heaven.

didn't get paid for my time—I didn't even get extra credit—but I happily volunteered to do it, giving up my own free period when I could have goofed off with friends my own age to instead act as a glorified babysitter to a bunch of strange little kids. I just wanted to get a taste at what being an authority figure was like, and I found that I loved it.

I admit that I played favorites during these times, though, just like how just a few years before, not an afternoon would go by when I wouldn't cluck my tongue against my teeth disapprovingly at an outburst Dylan made in my pretend classroom or over a barely passing grade he received on a math test. At the end of the year, I made up goodie bags for the kids in the *real* first grade class, filling small brown paper bags with candy, stickers, and Pogs, which were *really* in at the time, though we preferred to simply collect the *Beverly Hills 90210* or Scratch 'N Sniff ones we found at the corner candy store rather than actually play them against each other and risk losing any of our beloved cardboard tokens.

Anyway, when making up the bags, I found I had enough stuff left over for one more. I could have kept it for myself, or even given it to my best friend in my own class, but instead I decided to pick the one kid I liked best in the first grade class and give her "a little something extra." I probably should have at least done some sort of "fair drawing" if I was going to give it to one of those kids, so that my blatant favoritism wasn't so obvious, but I was still just a kid myself, and I couldn't see that. And I most certainly didn't expect kids who were a few years younger than me to see through it either!

Ironically— or quite fittingly, I guess, depending on how carefully you've been reading— the girl I favored in the first grade class was one who wanted to be an actress and had even auditioned for a big Hollywood film earlier in the year.[14] I had sat with her in the principal's office while she was waiting for her mom to come sign her out of school early for the audition and then held her hand as she

---

14 The film turned out to be *Striptease*.

walked down the stairs and out onto the street, wishing her luck, and probably silently wishing for her mom to take me with them. She didn't end up with the part,[15] but she was the kind of kid I just knew was going to go someplace. She was outgoing and confident and had a natural energy and magnetism that made everyone want to be her friend, including me, and I was four years older. She was my first personal brush with potential stardom, and once again, I found myself a bit envious of someone younger, so I did the one thing I knew how to do in order to ingratiate myself to her: I befriended her with special treatment. It's how I was being conditioned to believe the world worked, after all.

15 The role of Demi Moore's on-screen daughter went to Demi Moore's *real-life* daughter, Rumer Willis, instead.

SOMEBODY'S WATCHING (OVER) YOU...

I am a child of the eighties in that I was born in the eighties, not that said decade was the time I had my heyday. So being that I was so young then, I have been told I missed out on the wonders that were the "After School Specials." You may know the kind: Timmy had sex with his girlfriend for the first time and got her pregnant, and now he has to quit the JV baseball team and drop out of school to go get a job at some factory where he ends up losing three of the fingers on his pitching hand, and none of that ever would have happened if they had just abstained (or, you know, *used a condom*) in the first place. Sure, that kind of programming was around well into the early nineties, too, when I was finally old enough to appreciate the genre, but by then you could tell it was on its way out, as the production value diminished, despite advancing technology. Long gone were the days of gems like *Desperate Lives*, the one in which Helen Hunt takes PCP and jumps through a window! Instead we had to settle for the "Very Special Episodes" of insert-sitcom-here in order to learn the dangers of underage drinking/drinking and driving/experimenting with marijuana, which always— in the case of these shows— led to experimenting to methamphetamines. Or we could always just watch PBS.

Now as I approached my pre-teen years, I had to admit that nothing about PBS and the Children's Television Workshop that produced most of its content spelled "cool." They were a non-profit, which right away meant their programming was preachy and educational. By then my friends and I no longer played Pretty, Pretty Princesses or pretended our dolls and teddy bears were students in our classrooms, answering questions we recycled from our own tests and rewrote on the chalkboard in bedrooms or basements. In fact, we didn't really want to consider ourselves children anymore at all!

There was nothing appealing about the big purple dinosaur or the long lanky lamb that sang about loving you or songs that never end (respectively). Still, I would find myself at home on afternoons when the only other programming option for my seven-channel rabbit ears-tuned set box were reruns of cartoons I had seen a million times. And as much as I once loved *Duck Tales* or *Teenage Mutant Ninja Turtles*, I felt like I had equally grown out of them. So I would flick on PBS and listen with half an ear to the geographical trivia on *Where In The World Is Carmen San Diego?* And before I would realize it, it would be the start of a new half-hour and a new show, and suddenly my screen would be filled with a few hip, urban kids living in the same city I was, filling their afternoons not with the counting and spelling lessons of *Sesame Street* but with actual life lessons that they picked up on the streets— streets that were not too distant from my own block, I might add.

I'm going to ignore the fact that the original point to this show was simply to teach kids to read and write, just like *Sesame Street*, by the way, because I can still be just that hypocritical!

Ghostwriter featured a gang, for an ironic term, of kids who came together from different backgrounds because they had one very specific thing in common: they all had an invisible friend, or a ghost, if you're so inclined, who showed up at any moment he felt necessary and grabbed letters from anything nearby— clothes with logos, cereal boxes, old magazines— to spell out a Very Important Message. He never came by just to chat or to catch up and talk about their days at school; every time this aptly named Ghostwriter appeared, it was because someone in the nearby vicinity needed help, and he was going to give them that help through these enabling guinea pigs. And they relished it! Having probably been weaned on "Nancy Drew," "The Hardy Boys," and "The Babysitter's Club Mystery Specials" (just as I), these kids were itching to solve the puzzles Ghostwriter laid out in front of them.

Ghostwriter appeared in my home weekly, via the television of course, and really was its own self-contained after school special series. The dangers the kids faced were always ones you could imagine being right outside your own front door, and while growing up in New York City, that was often the more literal case. From gangs and graffiti taggers, to arson, to computer hackers, to the dumping of deadly chemicals in a community garden, the lesson was always firm: there is no gray area between what is right and what is wrong. If you know about some wrongdoing, it is just as much your responsibility to come forward and expose it as it is the wrongdoer's to confess.

In that way, *Ghostwriter* fit perfectly into the "scare your kids out of doing anything dangerous" tactics that our parents seemed to eat up. It also featured oddly religious overtones, as here was this invisible being that could (and often did) pop in on its select "chosen" few anytime it wanted and with special messages and visions solely for them. It not only helped to keep its street team, so to speak, in line when it came to all things moral, but it also trained its team to act as missionaries and spread the word of its teachings.

How I *sooo* yearned to be a part of *Ghostwriter*'s team! I scoured the pages of the Oriental Trading Company catalog for a non-bulk batch of pen-necklaces just like Alex, Jamal, Gaby, and Tina all sported. When I couldn't find one, and I couldn't convince my mother to spend almost thirty dollars on a box of one hundred, I even made my own for a little while, by simply hooking the pen to a piece of yarn by tucking the string under the cap. Not exactly foolproof, as the second I went to yank the pen out, the cap plummeted to the floor, but it would have to do.

I already carried around an old-fashioned marble notebook (though mine were always pink or purple for a little bit of individuality) in which I would jot stories as they came to me for my creative writing class, but I could easily spare a few pages for solving mysteries! And I tried to convince some of my friends to dedicate a section in the back of their matching ones for this supernatural detective work, too, but alas, none of them would have it. As children whose parents weren't censoring what they watched on television— and whose weren't cheap with a capital C and a capital HEAP— they all had cable and were spending their afternoons listening to *Clarissa Explain[s] It All* and scaring each other with recaps of the campfire stories from *Are You Afraid of the Dark?* I was the lone lookout in my third or fourth grade class for that spiraling stream of neon light.

Armed and ready to accept any message he would send me, I scanned my classroom almost compulsively, as I figured there would be the best place of any. With its stacks of textbooks and shelves of novels, not to mention the dozens of "inspirational" posters lining the walls, there were ample opportunities for letters to start flying around. But sadly, Ghostwriter never revealed himself to me.

Even though it must not seem like it, I was actually quite a big reader back then (and I still am!). It all started back in pre-school, when we had designated nap time in the middle of the afternoon, during which our teacher would instruct the class to get out our mats (or towels or giant pillows or with whatever our parents armed us at the beginning of the school year for just the occasion) and lie down on the floor. Everyone would be told to close their eyes as she snapped off the light and plopped down at her desk— for an upright nap of her own or a chance to catch up on the gossip magazines— and everyone would listen, utterly exhausted from the day of practicing the alphabet or Show and Tell or playing with the giant parachute. I was the lone wolf forced to stay at her desk, not allowed to take naps with the other kids during the designated time. My father gave my teachers the excuse that I had "severe dust allergies" and could not lie on the floor, but I think he was more paranoid about the germs I'd pick up in such close quarters to so many other sticky, sweaty little five year-olds.

So upright at my desk I sat, while everyone else went lights out. Though I probably should have put my head down and closed my eyes, too, that was just no fun unless someone was going to come around and slam my thumb down in a game of Seven Up. And after a day or so of just staring at the decorations on the wall, I quickly found that didn't cut it either, as that was how I spent the majority of the regular time in class anyway, and I had easily already memorized the drawings and stickers progress chart by now. My teacher encouraged me to entertain myself, so long as I did so quietly enough not to disrupt the few who actually dozed off during those few minutes.

So I did; I would bring my American Girl[16] books with me to occupy myself. At first, I just thumbed through, looking at the pictures, and possibly even making up some stories in my own head about what was going on with Samantha and all of her little friends, but slowly and surely I began to pick up the words on the page. It was actually my teacher who noticed I could read first, announcing it to my stunned parents during parent-teacher conference that quarter. They must have been thrilled: their daughter was *opting* for the boob tube when in fact she actually had other ways to entertain herself.

By the time *Ghostwriter* came on the air, I was already zipping through the assigned reading in school and not just because when it came time to read aloud, I would count the kids in front of me and then down the margins in the text to figure out which paragraph would come around to me. In second grade, my class had to take the first in a yearly tradition of statewide-standardized reading comprehension exams. At the halfway mark, my teacher had us all put our pencils down and stand at our desks, stretching out our arms and shaking out our legs. She was probably just trying to counteract the restless nature of our A.D.D. ridden generation, but it was welcome nonetheless, and when she called time to resume, I raised my hand

---

16 Which, by the way, I have to say were cool when I was a kid, but they were nothing then compared to how they are now. I mean; I had to cut and mismatch the old-timey clothes to try to make my Samantha doll "look just like me." Now they get their own hair salons, theatres, movies, and Dress Like Me outfits! Um, bitter? Party of one!

and said I was finished. She raised an eyebrow at me, told me that couldn't possibly be true, and implored me to check my work. I shrugged, not understanding what the big deal was: at this point I had *years* of reading under my belt, so I just assumed it was a given I would be good at it by now, and I rolled my pencil around my desk for the forty-five minutes that was left.

(In case you're wondering, I scored a 99 percentile on that test. And before you make the comment my father always did of "if you had studied more, you could have gotten the full 100%," let me point out that there was no perfect score on this type of test: 99% was it.)

It was right around that time that Judy Blume was becoming popular, and I admit I asked my mother to buy those when we went to the Walden Books in the Staten Island mall, too, but only to fit in with the girls in my class who were onto jeans and polo shirts when I still preferred stretch leggings and oversized Winnie The Pooh and Tweety Bird sweatshirts. In truth, those watered-down fictional stories seemed like they were better suited for someone growing up in the suburbs—or the seventies—than the hardened city kid that I was. And after a show like *Ghostwriter,* I yearned for more.

My mother had a rule when we went shopping in said mall: I was allowed to buy as many books as I wanted, as long I was continuing to enrich my mind through reading. It was a rule she sadly did not extend over to Macy's when I got old enough to enjoy going clothing shopping even though I clearly couldn't go to school naked!

Anyway, *Ghostwriter* gave me a taste for mysteries and the rush of potential threats, but I didn't believe I was invincible or immortal enough to withstand serious danger in my own life. So very quickly I began to gravitate towards the mysteries and threats of more supernatural, somewhat surreal tales. I was willing and able to suspend my disbelief for the time it took to read the stories, but then when I flipped the cover shut, I knew I sealed any danger up within the binding. I knew there were no such things as ghosts or monsters or possessed cars. But I was fascinated with the mind that could create things so outside the realm of reality.

Now, there comes a point in every young girl's life when she is faced with the possibility of a May-December romance. It's usually a thrilling feeling in its beginning stages— exhilarating even— that someone so young could have so much in common with a suave, sophisticated, downright *worldly* man. And let's face it: a little salt and pepper scruff hasn't hurt the likes of George Clooney or Patrick Fabian![17]

My own May-December moment came in the fourth grade, at the tender age of ten, when suddenly I put down my R.L. Stine books (because they were becoming a bit too *simple*, and he couldn't write them as fast I was reading them anyway) and started a love affair with the clean-cut, outdoorsy, yet speckled Stephen King. Or at least that's how he appeared on his book jacket, and I was smitten immediately.

Stephen and I— knowing nothing about him other than he wrote the first "adult" book that I ever read and with which miraculously managed to connect— were kindred spirits, I decided. I "got" him in a way I was sure no other girl my age could. If his fan mail address had been alongside Jonathan Taylor Thomas' or Mark-Paul Gosselaar's in Teen or Tiger Beat, I would have written love letters to *him* instead.

I guess every child goes through a phase where they realize they can't wait to just be a grown up[18] already, but that always felt much more like a true facet of my personality than just something that would come and go like a case of strep throat. By age ten I had already decided I liked some of my friends' parents more than I liked *them*. Often when I would go over to their houses, I would plant myself at the kitchen counter and attempt to engage the mothers in conversation. It was pretty clear that Barbie speak wasn't going to cut it, and somehow "So, those damn kids, huh?" didn't seem like

---

17 Professor Lasky, you have grown up so very nicely (*SBTB: The College Years*)!

18 "You know who don't use the term "grown-up?" Grown-ups!" – *Gilmore Girls*.

an appropriate opener either, so I turned my attention toward the one stereotypical thing I had seen suburban moms discuss at length, and I created my own one-on-one book club.

My best friend at the time had stacks upon stacks of well-worn paperback mysteries in her basement. I would gaze longingly and lovingly at them whenever she invited me over and we sat down there, working on a group project or playing video games. Looking through these stacks, I couldn't help but take note of the one name that seemed to pop up over and over: yes, one Mr. Stephen King. Eventually on a trip to the local bookstore with my mother, I armed myself with a copy of his "*It*," and perhaps thanks in part to our agreement about purchasing books, she didn't even blink an eye at what most might consider too mature a subject matter for such a young child. I kept the thousand-plus-page book on my windowsill, like a trophy, until it was time to head out to my then-best friend's house in the Hamptons.

Starting the read on the ride up, with the book pressed against the window to utilize as much of the streetlamp light spilling into the car as I could on the dark evening, I was instantly hooked. Even though I was just barely in double-digits, age-wise, I found I could greatly relate to the larger allegorical theme in the story. The clown was not just some Bozo with red hair and matching balloons: he was a symbol for the way their innocence was being stripped from them. A lot of little kids— my then-best friend's little brother included— are afraid of clowns because though they are supposed to bring happiness, they more often than not are somewhat shady, somewhat angry characters. A child who can see the cracks in their painted faces can see the truth. Unfortunately, this often has the same effect as finding out there is no Santa Claus: it causes the child to harden and become more self-aware. And once those things happen, they are no longer truly children.

The kids in "*It*" were living in a town full of abusers and injustice, things that also caused them to grow up much too soon. Though they were living in a different place and time, that theme was something I already understood. Sometimes the more a parent tries to shelter a child, the more the child realizes there are things wrong with the world in which they live. Such was the case for me, which was why I dove so deeply into various fictional worlds.

So I spent the majority of the trip with my nose in the novel—probably not being the most exciting houseguest my then-best friend's family ever had. I read before bed; I read early in the morning when I awoke before anyone else; I read lying on a lounge chair by the pool; I even read *in* the pool, balancing the book on the cement ledge, as I floated in the shallow end. I read after my shower when everyone else was taking their turns getting ready to go out to dinner, and I kept going until the glue binding of the cheap supermarket paperback had melted from the hot summer sun and pages were falling out by the handful.

On the day we were set to drive home, I sat in the kitchen while my then-best friend's mom made breakfast, and she asked me how I was enjoying the book. I smiled and pushed it across the counter to her, grinning cockily: "I loved it."

"You didn't finish it!" She exclaimed, shaking her head and writing me off immediately, as I had already come to learn most adults do with children. She wasn't asking; she was telling me I couldn't pull a fast one over her. It had only been two days, after all, and she, herself, probably hadn't even gotten through it so quickly.

"Yuh-huh," I replied earnestly and quite pleased with myself.

She stopped cooking momentarily to raise an eyebrow at me, and I'm sure I shrugged pretty smugly. She picked up the book and began leafing through it, presumably to see if the pages were worn with the sticky fingerprints to which kids my age were prone. Then she proceeded to ask me questions about the story, and not just the protagonists' names or the setting— not just the typical fourth grade book report stuff. She was virtually quizzing me, in disbelief that I did more than skim it and skeptical of how much I actually absorbed or understood. She asked me about those metaphors; she asked me why I thought the fears of the children were manifested in the form of a clown.

I passed her little test that day, and I felt oddly vindicated in doing so. Reading such a hefty work in such a short amount of time very quickly became my newest claim-to-fame. Somehow I felt like I didn't just pass a memory test or a comprehension test but also one of relate-ability: I was able to hold my own (at least it seemed that way to me at the time!) in an adult conversation. She took an interest— and the time— to have the kind of discussion I assumed all parents avoided. After all, if parents were willing to talk about these difficult subjects, wouldn't those After School Specials have no place in our society?

THEY CAN'T TAKE THAT (TV) AWAY FROM ME...

My friend Jamie nicknamed my father Michael Chiklis because when he shaved his head she thought they resembled each other. He thinks so, too. He revels in it, in fact. It's kind of funny because if I were still a young child now, the reference would be lost on me. *The Shield* is not a show that he would have allowed me to watch.

If you've ever heard the term "heard around the water cooler" you know a few things. One, it's out dated! I'm going to be the type of mother whose kids look at her and say she's old. Not even necessarily for my numerical age, but because of how I grew up: I was around during a time when computers were not a staple in every household, cell phones and internet were for the rich businessmen only, and there were no CD players, MP3s, or DVDs. I honestly still don't quite know what we did back then!

But also you can automatically remember the things that were popular enough to be discussed in such a place. *Melrose Place, The Simpsons, Dallas, 30 Something, Married With Children...* shows that spoke to generations of people. Shows that had the potential to become classics— and some that actually made it to that status— because they stirred something within their audiences. They were relatable, but most importantly, they were often *controversial*; they got people talking, and in turn, that got even more people interested in them. These shows were chock full of new spins on old ideas— witty, clever, creative, unique...and for me, *verboten.*

Even in elementary school, we had a water cooler of sorts: it was called the schoolyard. Every morning my group of friends and I would gather and talk about the coolest music (New Kids on the Block), cutest boys (Mark-Paul Gosselaar and J.T.T.), and what we watched on television the night before. And that's where we all varied. Though I was allowed to buy the NKOTB cassettes with all of my other little girlfriends—hell, I even had the complete set of trading cards and some buttons to match! —for some reason, my mother drew the line at owning the Jordan doll that would have gone so nicely with my fashionista Barbie. I mean, who better to date a singer than a model, right? But no. To this day, I don't know if my mother nixed the doll idea because she feared they might be anatomically correct or what—the last time I asked her, she claimed she didn't even remember saying no when I asked for one for Christmas or my birthday. But she must have, because I never found it under the tree or in a stocking. It was just one more thing in the long line of fads in which I was not allowed to partake. Super ironically now, television just held the majority of those examples.

I must have had a bedtime back then, but I don't remember what it was. It was probably during primetime, at some point, but even then it was a tentative plan at best. More often than not, even if I made it into my bed at the appropriate time, I could still hear the television through my bedroom wall, which was simply a louver door (the kind that slides open and has slots in it so sight and sound carry in long thin slits), and I would lie awake longer than I should have, straining to make out the dialogue in shows that were strictly off-limits. I didn't get a television in my bedroom until I was about eleven or twelve, and I didn't get a real *door* for another four years after that. Sometimes I still wonder why I never called Child Protective Services about that...

To be honest, I'm not quite sure what my parents were so worried about me picking up from television: when I was three years old and riding in my car seat in the back of his old Buick, my mother tells me a car cut us off, and I yelled out "*@$$hole*!" as we swerved around the guy. Apparently I had already been learning enough from my father. How badly could television screw me up??

For my friends, the current obsession at one point was a combination of *The Simpsons* and *Married With Children* (later they got into *90210*, too, but oddly I never cared enough about that one to fight for viewing rights). Kids would come into school bursting to talk about the latest funny thing Kelly Bundy said, or what Bart Simpson referenced that they didn't quite understand but maybe one of the rest of us did. The thing about that kind of humor is that most of it goes over the heads of little kids anyway.

In the episode of *Friends* "Where Ross and Rachel...You Know," they're kissing on the museum floor, and she stops him abruptly and says: "*Oh, honey, that's okay,*" and he tells her that he just rolled over the juice box. Well, I was ten when that first aired, and without sex education in my New York City public elementary school, I had never heard the term "premature ejaculation" before (and my life was simpler for it!), so I just assumed she thought he had accidentally peed on her. Yes, seriously.

Yet my father still feared it would cause me to grow up before my time. Thus it was banished from me. So he would sit in the living room alone, cackling heartily, as I feigned sleep, attempting to imagine the faces that went along with the few words I could make out. When one of my good friends went as Peg Bundy for Halloween when we were ten years old, I even had to pretend not to know who she was so my parents wouldn't get suspicious.

When I was a kid I was closer with my father's sister than anyone else, and because of it, I would often visit her and her husband for a week at a time, even without my own parents. They would drop me off—maybe spend the Easter or Christmas holiday with us—and then come back a few days later—a few days after I had gotten my share of freedom, I guess. They probably figured it was the safest place to leave me, though, considering my aunt and my uncle were über-conservative, and they lived in a big house tucked nearly away in suburbia, where I could play outside in the snow all by myself and never have to worry about a strange car pulling up and the driver trying to coax me inside with candy or a puppy, which was, perhaps, my father's second greatest fear, right behind what I might pick up from television.

My uncle loved his cop dramas. He watched them religiously, with a glass of wine in one hand and the "clicker" in the other so that no one would change the channel—even during the commercials. His all time favorite show at the time was *NYPD Blue*, or as my father liked to call it: *gratuitous fucking*—both for the language and the reference to seeing Dennis Franz' ass. Needless to say, *that* show was not permitted in my house, either, and sitting with my uncle, unaware of who anybody was or what was going on, I suddenly understood why my mother always made me invite the one moody girl in my class who no one really got along with to my birthday parties. Because while she never really seemed to want to be there and would choose to sit alone in the corner and pout the whole time, she probably felt better on the inside (even if she didn't show it) that she had been included in the first place. She would know what everyone was talking about in the schoolyard the next morning, and that knowledge alone was a little bit of power. It made her privy to things that some others still weren't, and it made her one of the cool kids, too.

My uncle let me stay up and watch the show with him, and although he probably would have taken the time to explain the situations to me if I had asked, I never needed him to. I was hooked from the first scene in which Jimmy Smits hauled ass down some dark, dirty New York City alleyway after a perp., and I sat on the edge of the couch with my chin in my hands, soaking up every word. Should it be a surprise, then, that in high school, when I went on my screenplay writing kick, they were all crime thrillers? Not if you've been paying attention! *NYPD Blue* was just the tip of the iceberg; I did not even previously know I had an interest in finding out what was behind the door that it opened for me.

I still don't know how my father found out about our little screenings—maybe I accidentally let it slip that I couldn't wait to see if Jimmy and Kim Delaney finally got together, as I was convinced was only inevitable from the longing way they looked at each other over case files and stale cups of coffee. But he did, and he called my uncle, screaming like a lunatic and threatening to never let me visit again. If he was only trying to protect me from seeing Dennis Franz' naked behind, then I guess I can't really fault him too much, but let's face it, he's just not that caring!

My uncle probably assumed I was the snitch because the next time I visited, instead of just holding his finger to his lips and telling me it would be our little secret, I was sent up to the guest room promptly at ten p.m., so he could enjoy the show alone. I, on the other hand, lay awake well into the hour creating my own, albeit somewhat sophomoric, episode plotlines in my mind.

When I was eleven and twelve, I spent a lot of weekends during the summer months going out to the Hamptons with my then-best friend's family. Her father had built a house out there when we were small, and usually he would rent it out to other families during the summer, so that he would have some extra income to pay for his four children's college education. But for a brief moment in middle school, he began to use the house again, and I was the chosen token friend who could come along for the ride.

My then-best friend's mom loved Broadway shows, especially *Rent*. She played the soundtrack in the car all of the time, only skipping over one song[19]— her own version of censorship, I guess. That summer, though, listening to the songs in the back of an old Ford Explorer plowing down bumpy country roads, I was on the edge of my seat—literally, sitting with my chin in my hands, straining to hear the

19 Disc 2, Song #9: "Contact".

lyrics over the whining and fighting about who lost the Super Mario Brothers cartridge for the Gameboy of my then-best friend and her little brother. I came home knowing the entire book by heart and singing the melodies from memory. I begged my mother to buy me the soundtrack, too, so I could listen to it whenever I wanted. I had been moved in a way I had never been before.

Roger and Mimi's combativeness in "Another Day" perfectly depicted what I was battling within myself on a daily basis, desperate to balance my rationality and logical thinking with my emotional nature. Could I adopt the "live in the moment" attitude I so admired from a true Bohemian or was I destined to be a constant worrier, desperate to set myself up now for a future that may never even come?

I greatly admired the carefree joy of "La Vie Boheme," yelling along at the top of my lungs with the names of those incomparable creatives and yearning to be one of them. When Anthony Rapp sang, *"Is anyone in the mainstream?"* I couldn't stop the tears from welling up in the corners of my eyes; that single line summed up exactly how I wanted to be comfortable to live. During years when I could not feel more different, here were some other young people just living their lives and happy to do so in the way they wanted to: they didn't think they were the outsiders, and they were genuinely confused by the idea of "the masses."

"What You Own" made me want to rebel against my upper middle class mother's way of buying my love; I was both Mark and Roger arguing over giving into emotion and running from it so as not to get hurt in the middle of "Good-Bye Love;" and I painfully understood "One Song Glory" and "Santa Fe" and that deep desire to be somewhere great and to do something great, just to leave your mark on this world as it chews you up but before it spits you back out.

Jonathan Larson had seduced me. I can't say I ever found him physically attractive, but he had seduced my mind and my heart. He was like the big brother a little girl grew up idolizing and then spent the majority of her adult life trying to find a boyfriend who made her feel a similar way. Okay, admittedly, I have always found this a bit creepy...but not more so than when people say little girls grow up to marry guys like their fathers. To me, *that* is much worse!

My mother indulged me and purchased the soundtrack, but she still wouldn't let me see the play. She and my father thought I was too young for the content; somehow they had convinced themselves that I had never been exposed to sex or drugs or disease before, and they wanted to shield me (the "impressionable" pre-teen) from it, effectively trying to shield me from life.

I never quite understood it: I already knew what the play was about by hearing the soundtrack. What could be so much worse about the visuals?

As it turns out, nothing. If anything, seeing the performers jump around on stage with so much passion and conviction just made the words that much stronger, and in that, probably lies what my parents were truly so worried about: they saw me embracing a way of life they did not understand, let alone condone. But it was reality, and more importantly, it was *my* reality.

Like the characters in *Rent*, I was living in New York, trying to pursue a career in the arts (film, just like the story's narrator, Mark). I saw the homeless people depicted on stage everyday— hanging outside of McDonald's for some spare change, pushing supermarket carts full of scraps of magazine and old tee shirts, and diving into garbage cans for empty bottles. I had already had my introduction to drugs when, in the fourth grade, one of the local high school dealers made his way onto my elementary school's playground—probably under the guise of being someone's older brother—and offered a classmate tabs of something I assume was LSD because of the rumors that had been swirling that in order to get younger and younger kids hooked, some of the temporary tattoos that had become so popular, and we being sold for a quarter in supermarket gumball machines, were laced.

When I was fourteen, and Kids Night on Broadway time came around again, offering free seats to those under a certain age, my mother relented, coaxed by my then-best friend's mom who was bringing her own daughter to the show. So we all went together. It was after the original cast had dismantled and only a few stragglers were left, and the experience was still one-of-a-kind and indescribable, as it was my de-virginizing of Broadway in general. Still, a part of me still couldn't help but say: *"That was it?"* as I walked out of the theater. It wasn't that I didn't love every minute of it even more than when I was just listening through headphones on the bus on my way to school (because I *did*), but my parents had made it seem like it was "way too mature" for me for so long that I expected it to be a lot more controversial when actually it was pretty much like everyday life. Lyrically brilliant, poetic, and moving…but still just everyday life. And of that, perhaps my parents should have been most afraid.

Because that's the thing about censorship: the more you tell someone they can't do something, the more they want to do it, and it usually turns out that they create something a lot worse in their minds than what the thing turns out to really be. So the bar for shock value keeps being raised because of all of those people who were expecting one thing but end up getting another, and they end up even more desensitized than if they had just been allowed to see the original thing in the first place without all of the fuss.

A few years ago, I read article in Time Magazine that was talking about television going too far in terms of obscenity. One man was quoted as saying he wished things could just go back to how they were in the 50s. *"Things were better in the 50s. The 50s this and the 50s that; the 50s were not corrupt."* Um, newsflash, mister: the 50s were not so different than life in 2005—which was when I read the article—except that in the 50s, everything was repressed. No one talked about homosexuality, infidelity, or impotence, but they were all still there. Interracial relationships, homophobia, racism, and illiteracy: everything we still grapple with today was present then, too. It was just hidden behind cookie-cutter white-picket fences where women wore frilly aprons while baking cookies (from scratch!) and awaiting their husbands' return home from work so maybe they would get that brand-new washer/dryer with his hard-earned paycheck. And if that man wants to live in the ignorance brought on by his own mind's censorship, let him. But it won't be bliss.

I often wonder if the man quoted in that article was just my father, under a pseudonym. I'd hate to think such archaic thinking still widely exists.

There's a group in the south (also something I learned from this Time article) who spend their days watching prime time programming from nights prior and keeping a list of any time an obscenity is in place. There are categories: cursing, nudity, murder, adultery, etc. They create Excel spreadsheets that carefully list the date, program, episode number, and instance. For example, an episode of *CSI* could get a mention because it showed shadowy figures having a threesome in a seedy Las Vegas hotel room. These people are the Indecency Police (something I have deemed them—not something they actually respond to), and they post form letters on the Internet so other "outraged" citizens can sign their names to petitions to silence such atrocities. If these people are able to prosper on a larger scale, and if the demands in their letters are actually met, then virtually every program will be pulled from the airwaves. I don't know what the resulting new shows would be like, and quite frankly, I don't want to know!

Back in the day, my parents might have found a very rewarding career with these people. In the end, such behavior clearly backfired on my parents, though, as I found ways around their rules time and time again, and I now watch so much television a friend from college once told me "it makes [his] eyes bleed." To that, that is one of my crowning achievements, and I guarantee that a large chunk of it would be shows of which neither my mother nor my father would approve.

BE CAREFUL WHAT YOU WISH FOR...

My sixth grade social studies teacher gave me the endearing—or insulting, depending on where you're coming from, I guess— nickname of a "pizza bagel" because my father was Italian Catholic and my mother, Jewish. I, on the other hand, liked to think of myself as "mixed"— just like my childhood idol, Ms. Mariah Carey— though I knew that wasn't really an appropriate term.

Mariah came from biracial parents, but I thought bi-*religious* parents could be just as challenging, if not controversial. One time after reading an article in which Mariah opened up that this often happened in her white mother and African American/Venezuelan father's house, I even threw a rock through our window screen, trying to convince my parents that our middle class old-fashioned neighbors must have had a problem with their "alternative lifestyle."

If my parents noticed that the screen bended outward, toward the street, instead of into our apartment, they kept it to themselves. If my parents understood that the bending of the screen in fact proved the direction of the projectile was actually the opposite of how it should have been if the culprit (i.e.: rock-thrower) really was a disapproving neighbor, they let it go. They repaired— not even replaced— the broken screen without saying a word to me about how it got that way in the first place. They also ignored the fact that there was no rock lying accusatorily on the living room floor. Hell, they never used to notice when I'd slip my peas and carrots into a napkin in my lap and then make multiple in-the-middle-of-dinner trips to the bathroom to flush said napkins' contents down the toilet instead of consuming them, so needless to say, C.S.I.s they most certainly were not!

Anyway, my seemingly unique background made for quite a few, shall we say, "boisterous discussions" over the years over everything from the fact that my maternal grandparents constantly sent religious cards instead of the pagan rituals my father's side of the family had adopted, to the fact that my love of tattoos meant I couldn't get buried in a Jewish cemetery. It equally allowed my parents to take a backseat in the religious education department, though— something which they were quite eager to do considering they were taking a backseat in every other education department. They preferred to assume my overcrowded public schooling would be enough for me to become a contributing member of society. After all, my dad claimed he only got an 804 on the SATs—and he seemed oddly proud of that— so there wasn't a whole lot to which their baby girl had to live up anyway!

My parents' educational complacency started when I was in first grade and my school sent home a permission slip asking parents to enroll their children in a sex education class within regular school hours. Parents, if approving of the program, would sign the form and return it with their child by a certain day so the class could start immediately. Anyone who didn't turn the form in, or whose parents didn't want them learning such things from someone other than themselves, would be given special projects or a book to read or simply told to turn around and face the corner until the lesson was done.

Now, my elementary school did this every year following that first attempt until we graduated in the fifth grade, without ever actually giving us the class. I guess our teachers were just as lazy as my parents.

Or maybe those permission slips only started to placate parents after a first grade classmate of mine brought in one of those "Where Do Babies Come From?" books[20] that featured nude cartoons—which

20 The exact book was "Where Do I Come From?" by Arthur Mayle. These days they offer many more options, including ones designed for girls, ones for boys, ones for adopted kids, and ones for kids with two same-sex parents. The illustrations feature every ethnicity and even different age groups. But back when I was a kid, all we had was this one that taught you sex was for fat, old people.

by the way, I thought too-closely resembled by own aunt and uncle and might explain why I was so disinterested in sex years later!

This girl passed the book around the class, and by the end of the day I had traced one of the illustrations of the woman, telling my friends I was sure it would be the perfect gift to give another little first grader in our class for his upcoming birthday. I was quite the expert tracer back then, too; I didn't even need special paper—just a sheet of loose leaf and a pencil and the original image, and I could recreate any photo or drawing masterpiece. I thought I was pretty clever, but my teacher was not nearly as amused. I assume a note was sent home because my mother bought the same book and actually attempted to give me "the talk" shortly thereafter. Or at least, she started to.

My mother called me into her bedroom and shut the door so that I had nowhere to which to escape while she read a book with which I was already more than familiar. I was six; all I wanted to do was watch *Tiny Toons*. I don't really remember her trying to explain anything as she read— just that her tone of voice was as it would be for "Goodnight Moon" or "Give A Mouse A Cookie" or "Eloise." She basically read verbatim and kind of nodded at the photos, as if they offered all of any additional information I might need. I remember getting really bored and uncomfortable and finally just telling her I had to pee so I could storm out of the room. I never went back in, and she didn't press the issue. She never brought it up again, even when she probably should have, and I was left still scratching my head at the enigma that was sex until quite a few years later.

And so I entered the halls of junior high naïve and ill-prepared for the onset of puberty that inevitably faced my friends and me.

It's hard to say exactly to whom—or what—my parents were leaving the parenting up. Often it seemed like they just assumed I would turn out fine based on some sort of super genetics they had passed down to me. Just like how they didn't want to be bothered explaining birds and the bees to me, they didn't want to tackle the tough—and more often than not, controversial—topic of religion, either. So while they each had one they belonged to by default of their own upbringing, I was left somewhere in the middle—with nothing and nowhere to fit in.

While the other little Catholic boys and girls in my elementary school class would line up by the coat closet in the middle of the afternoon every Wednesday, packed and ready to jump ship—err, *leave school*—early, I still sat with my hands not-so patiently folded on top of my desk. They got bussed off to C.C.D. to study for their communions, and later their confirmations, which in my mind were just excuses to wear frilly white dresses (something in which I was not interested at all) and get lots of checks from relatives they've never met before (something in which I had an increasingly piquing interest), while I had to remain with only a handful of other kids and finish out the day.

The handful of other kids were Jewish—except maybe for one or two who were Lutheran or Greek Orthodox or something equally foreign that no one had bothered to explain to me. So we sat on those Wednesday afternoons in some kind of solidarity, knowing we would never have to eat stale wafers or drink what we were told was dead man's blood. But the ones who were there were the good and proper kind who went to religious schools on their own time and studied for their own parties of equal importance. And then the cheese stood alone. Or in my case, the pizza bagel.

I didn't think much about religion until I was in junior high, but I think I always felt like I was missing out on something. Like Ariel, I guess I, too, yearned to be "a part of [that] world." You know, the grass is always greener and all that. By junior high, my real questioning was beginning. There are mid-life crises; there are even quarter-life crises; but there was no term that I had found then (or since) for what I was experiencing.

Though my parents said I could choose whether I wanted to be a Catholic or a Jew when I was old enough to make those big, important decisions for myself, they never gave me any foundation on which to do so. And they never told me *when* I would be old enough or *how* I could make such a big, important decision if I had no background or frame of reference on either religion (or *any* religion, for that matter). So while my friends went off to keg parties in park by the all boys' Catholic high school (the irony not lost on me even then!), I turned to what I had already come to think of as my bible and began a little training of my own.

Julianne Morris, too, was on *Days of our Lives* in the mid-nineties.[21] Though her character was kind of one-note (literally in the beginning when she was playing mute: a woman who had grown up in a swamp without any human contact), the actress herself was a walking dichotomy. The daughter of a Baptist minister who vowed to remain a virgin until marriage, despite her devout beliefs, she was working in a town and an industry that sold sex.

Julianne spoke openly and freely of her faith—one just had to know where to look, and thankfully (or perhaps by the grace of a God I didn't yet quite understand), by the time she started on *DOOL,* I was already knee-deep in such texts thanks to my slightly unhealthy obsession with one Mr. Jensen Ackles.

Every Friday after school I would stop at one of the newsstands on my route home. There were at least half a dozen, and if I popped into one, and they didn't have the newest issue of Soap Opera Magazine or Soap Opera Update,[22] I could try the one on the next corner. Every third Tuesday, I'd also make a stop at Rite Aid to pick up the special edition NBC Soaps issue, as well. Those became my bibles just as much as my television set, and in them I found words to live by in order to get everything that I thought I wanted out of life.

---

21 Maybe some of these stories should have been saved for a sequel memoir called "My Days With *Days*!"

22 Both now as defunct as those old Sterling Press teen magazines.

In one such interview, Julianne said that it wasn't right for everyone, and "it [wasn't] always easy, but [she was] waiting." I was intrigued. Here was a beautiful, *adult* woman who managed to attract some equally beautiful *adult* men, with both her feet planted firmly on the ground. She would stick to her guns—and her morality— at any cost, but she didn't come off as the dorky Donna Martin for doing so. Somehow Julianne just blindly trusted in an unknown force that everything would work out and that she would find someone who would understand and respect her beliefs, if not believe in the same things. That was something I was sorely missing. And something in that just clicked for me; you're only as good as your examples, and she was mine.

By the time I turned fourteen, with a solid...oh, I don't know, four or five months of this kind of religious study under my belt, I thought I had it all figured out. I knew who I was, what I believed, and perhaps most importantly, what I wanted and who I wanted to be in life. So I, too, made a vow, and I solidified it with a heart-shaped charm inscribed with the words: "True Love Waits" that I attached to my key ring. It became quite the trendy act once Britney Spears, a few years later, declared herself a virgin until marriage, too. Suddenly, those rings and heart necklaces were being purchased and worn like Best/Friends charms: intermittently and only to accessorize certain, specific outfits. Just like a part of my decision probably came from the desire to be more like Julianne, hundreds of little girls "took the vow" to be more like Britney. My innately cynical nature can only assume that once Britney broke it, so did they...if they even still remembered by that point that they had done so at all. And thanks to the Jonas Brothers, I am sure the cycle has started all over again.

At the time, though, I figured it was the only logical thing that I could do if I wanted to ensure I was surrounded by good quality people, though. If someone didn't respect my beliefs, they didn't deserve my respect, friendship, or *any* place in my life, really. In a way, Julianne had given me a valid excuse and the "it's okay" I felt I needed to put off something for which I felt I wasn't ready; she allowed me to hide behind a religion I didn't full yet understand (let alone fully subscribe to) just to cover some of my own insecurities and oddities.

Freshman year of college brought a ton of changes, but oddly enough, my vow did not falter—though at that point it was more about wanting to keep a promise to *myself* rather than a higher being I wasn't entirely sure even existed anymore. Instead of following my floor-mates to house parties on frat row, I opted for "safer" activities, like volunteering at the on-campus television station, dive-in movie night, and spending an ungodly amount of time tanning and watching the men's polo team practicing in the Olympic sized pool.

I started seeing Choir Boy after meeting him at one such movie night mixer aimed at getting us newbs out of the comfort of our own dorm walls and mingling with others across campus. We had a friend in common—someone who had noticed the charm on my key ring and had raised an eyebrow but never said anything disparaging—and we ended up standing in a corner, away from the crowd, talking and laughing until we didn't even notice our mutual friend had broken away, and it was just the two of us who were actually getting along so well.

Choir Boy and I were on different paths, professionally, so we never had any classes together and were rarely even on the same side of campus at the same time. Still, he'd call me when he knew I was in between lectures, walking to the next one, or just killing time with a smoothie and a book on a bench by the big fountain in the quad. We spent countless nights watching movies in the dark of my apartment or going out to off-campus dinners in the luxury of his sedan. Choir Boy was always a gentleman, holding my hand through credits and stoplights alike. In fact, sometimes I though he was a little *too* gentlemanly. Though I wasn't thinking of jumping into bed at the time, I was really taken aback when *he* didn't try anything. And I mean *aaaannny*thing.

We were about three months into our relationship, and a week or two away from visiting his parents at their valley family home for the start of the holiday season, and he had barely even kissed me.

Okay, let me clarify a little: Choir Boy had kissed me in that he had given me pecks on the cheek or forehead or lips—but he hadn't *kissed* me kissed me. It was odd, and I definitely thought something was up there, but I had sort-of asked for it. I always said I wanted someone who wasn't going to pressure me to do anything I wasn't ready to, and maybe I was just giving off signals that I wasn't ready to do *any*thing. And I mean *aaaannny*thing.

On the car ride to Choir Boy's parents' house, which turned out to be over an hour in length due to heavy— but which I have since learned is just typical— traffic, I thought it would be the perfect time to bring it up. Because, you know, even if it spurred an argument, we'd have more than enough time to break up and get back together before exiting the freeway! So I reached out to lower Jay-Z on the stereo and turned to him as we crawled along the 10.

"So what's the deal with us?" I heard myself ask but still couldn't quite believe it. I always talked a good game, but when it came to relationships I was pretty passive. "I mean, are we really dating or what?"

Choir Boy laughed and said that of course we were, and that if I had to question it, we might have a problem.

I sighed and turned to stare into the driver's window of the minivan adjacent to his Nissan. "Well, it's kind of hard to know. I mean, I like hanging out with you and all, but you've never made a move. We haven't even kissed."

Choir Boy didn't accuse me of never making a move either. No one ever usually accuses me of anything. I still haven't quite figured out why that is. Maybe they're afraid of me or something; maybe they think I'll snap when faced with confrontation, and they'll end up missing a finger or toe or slightly more important extremity. Or maybe he just didn't want to be a hypocrite. I was far less concerned with such things.

"No, but I thought you were cool with all that. I mean, I thought you were waiting, too. You told Jess you were."

Okay, I had never actually explained to our mutual friend—or anyone, for that matter— the true meaning of my keychain. While it may have been something of a fad for many—not unlike my own long forgotten Tamagotchi—for me it was something I held onto quite deeply and quite seriously, even if only to hide behind. For me, it wasn't just about feeling connected to someone or even something bigger than just another person. It wasn't about being married to God or anything. It was a simple way to tell guys *"Hands off; I'm not ready just yet"* without having to explain too much of the why behind it. Because if I thought guys wouldn't like to hear no, I *knew* they'd like the therapy session that came with the reasoning *far* less.

The "too" in his words caught my attention, though.

"The thing is," he started, "my faith is really important to me. I feel like being a good Christian is the most important thing I can be, above being a good son or student or boyfriend. Actually, that's not entirely true: I think being a good Christian *makes* me better at all of those things. And to me, being a good Christian is remaining pure—as pure as the day I was born—until my wedding night. Because that is the best gift I can give my wife."

Huh.

It sounded like something straight out of a Lifetime movie or after-school special, and I don't know why I was so surprised, but I was, though I guess I had asked for *this*, too. The Secret works, you guys! But just like in the *Supernatural* episode "Wishful Thinking," getting what I thought I wanted backfired in a big way.

The funny thing is, it always appears to be an extreme with me, and though I always said I wanted a boyfriend who would respect and try to understand where I was coming from when it came to my issues with intimacy, I somehow never expected to find one who took it one step even farther than I did! I don't think I really expected that there were any of them left—well, not those whose voices had already dropped anyway. And I found it made me slightly uncomfortable. Because it made me feel like a fraud.

"So is this going to be a problem for you?"

His question hung in the air for a few seconds, while I could only shake my head a bit numbly and think of all I had vowed, too. I suddenly felt like as big a hypocrite as I judged Britney Spears to be. After all, it wasn't for some deep religious faith that I had come to find spirituality but still just that sophomoric way of looking up to someone famous to guide my way through life. And hearing someone speak of his devotion so seriously just made me feel like a giant ass.

Choir Boy and I ended up breaking up just a few weeks later. I wish I could say it ended amicably, and we're still friends— actual friends who still each other at parties or go out to lunch to catch up and not just Facebook friends who once in awhile see each other's new status pop up in our news feeds. Unfortunately, though, that isn't the case. I hadn't grown up much since the days of breaking up over IM—at least not when it came to things of this nature.

With Choir Boy, I took the "distant" route in order to end things. I started to find ways to be too busy to hang out with him as much as we had been. In my defense, it wasn't entirely untrue; I was prepping for a much busier second semester of college than my first had been— with a new internship, more class units, and some new friends from outside our shared circle.

I wasn't trying to be cold or calculating in anyway. I wasn't the stereotypical college kid just looking to get laid who broke up with someone simply because they wouldn't put out. I greatly respected his decision; I just realized his decision was not truly mine. I was no longer waiting until marriage...because I now knew I never wanted to get married.

But maybe that's a whole other story.

I didn't want Choir Boy to feel like he was wasting his time with me if he was ultimately working toward that "end," and since I could already hear the argument in my mind of *"If you love me, why don't you want to get married?" "Well, if* ***you*** *love me, why can't you respect how I feel?"* I figured it would just be better (and easier) for us both if we went our separate ways sooner rather than later.

Besides, a part of me wasn't sure we'd be able to get through the holiday season with a good ratio of the religious and the Hallmark traditions!

All right, all right, yes I am very good at making excuses and finding faults or "outs" in relationships. Even though it seemed I might have found all I had said I was looking for those so many years ago when I made the vow, I still ran. I still didn't believe it could work out. I still convinced myself we still weren't "meant to be" or whatever because our beliefs weren't *exactly* the same.

And *yes*, I realize just how hypocritical it was of me to break up with him for the same reasons I thought guys would want to dump *me*. I am nothing if not an enigma.

I took that TLW charm off my key ring when Choir Boy and I broke up to avoid any future confusion. I thought about giving it to him as somewhat of a memento but thought that also could be pretty easily misconstrued, so in the end I opted just to tuck it into a photo box I used to hold keepsakes from my childhood. If nothing else, I hoped whenever I'd go back through that box, I'd see it and remember my time with both him and Julianne. And maybe I'd finally learn something from my *own* actions—or inaction, as it were—for a change!

As odd as it may seem, or depending on your point of view, perhaps ironic—in that Alanis Morissette sort of way— the year after

I graduated from college I found myself dating another guy who shared similar beliefs as Choir Boy's. Though this new guy wasn't a virgin, he had become newly celibate. Not quite born again but close enough for my book, this guy actually explained his motives in terms I could understand: he was an actor, and he just found it too easy to get sucked into the corruption that ran rampant all over this industry and town. It was his way of getting control over at least one situation and taking a little part of himself back and keeping it close until he was sure he was with someone genuine and good. I not only held great admiration for that, but it was also something to which I could definitely relate.

THE GAY PIN-UP AND THE TWENTY-SOMETHING VIRGIN...

I have been told I have a "type," and that type is the gay pin-up. You know the guy; you've seen him on your local Armani billboard (think about those David Beckham or Cristiano Ronaldo ads...I know I am!). He's chiseled and handsome with just a hint of ruggedness. If he's blond, he's dirty blond and wears it cut close to his scalp; if he has a baby face, he hides it with a day or two of scruff; and if he's metro, he still has skulls, not polo guys, on his collared shirts. He's the kind of guy of whom sexually confused boys all over the world keep photos hidden between the pages of a ne'er-used Playboy. He's the kind of guy of whom those boys, when grow up or move out and are no longer "confused," pin those same photos up on their dorm room walls or Secret boards. He's the kind of guy on the cover of GQ and Details: he has pretty, feminine features but does what he can to "butch up." He's the kind of guy, therefore, who is "just gay enough," to quote Toby Young a bit.

Even now, I can hear the light bulbs clicking on in your minds. I bet this explains Jensen, Mark-Paul, and Tan Man—all of those I've mentioned in the past— and all of those I will undoubtedly mention in the near future.

I never really noticed it before—in fact, if asked directly, I always say I don't have a type at all as long as the guy has nice arms, a nice smile, nice eyes, is taller than me (at 5'6," I don't think that's too much to ask!), and isn't too hairy—oh, now I see!

...Maybe this explains why I fall in and out of love so quickly with actors but have so few boyfriends that live outside of my HD flat-screen. Seriously, my old blog entries read like some schoolgirl's diary: "I found my future husband;" "It's no wonder why I love him;" "He's so pretty it hurts" are all actual headlines. I have committed to print and then rewritten my Top Five List[23] more times than my formal-math-education-stopping-at-calculus will allow me to count.

Mark Wahlberg, in his infamous CK billboards (or any photo you may have snapped of him stripping down to his tightie whities during a performance as the lead of the Funky Bunch) was—and in many ways, still *is*— a prime example of such a guy. Taped up in lockers, next to vanities, on ceilings, or in the case of Kathy Geiss,[24] on the walls of a major television network's corporate office, Wahlberg consumed every waking moment of thought and was often the first thing you saw when you woke up in the morning and the last you did before you fell asleep— in those cases where he was splayed and *dis*played on the ceiling, anyway. But with my conservative parents, I had to settle for the much less threatening but still adorable Jonathan Taylor Thomas.

Back when Sterling Magazines boasted half a dozen variations on Tiger Beat (Um, Teen Beat, Big Bopper, 16, Super Teen, where did you guys go???), JTT, as we all affectionately called him, permanently owned at least an inch of the cover space on every issue. While the "articles" inside would always be more of the same "What's your favorite color/food/animal" questionnaires, the glossy photos would inevitably vary. Sometimes we'd be given a full page or two (the worst was when both sides of one page was a shot of JTT, and I'd have to spend another four bucks of a not-so-hard-earned allowance just so I could hang *both* on my walls), but when we were really lucky, we'd get a pull-out poster the size of *four* full pages.

---

23 You know, the list of the five celebrities you're allowed to sleep with and your significant other can't get mad. Then again, I guess I'd have to have an actual boyfriend before I can make that list, but you know, *semantics*!

24 30 *Rock* Season 3, Episode 1: "Do Over".

Each sheet got carefully torn out of the simple staple binding and hung up in a carefully chosen spot in my bedroom until every inch of the aged, baby pink paint had been covered with makeshift wallpaper. At one point, I had to start overlapping or risk being forced to remove some of the older, slightly faded but still adorable head shots. And if I could have reached the ceiling, I would have started in on that, too.

From as early as I can remember, I was enamored by the pretty, pretty people who made their way into my life and my home via the slightly-rounded black box at which all of my furniture was pointed. I never really expected to see any so much beauty in person, and I didn't...until I moved out to Los Angeles the summer after I graduated from high school.

Maybe it was the switch in coasts: in New York we were pale and beady-eyed from scurrying like vermin underground in order to travel around the city, but in L.A. we are tanned and somehow toned, despite sitting in traffic for triple the amount of time we may have to dedicate to the gym. Maybe it was because I went to a math and science magnet high school—or maybe it was because I had just come out of high school in general—where the boys were lanky and knobby-kneed and well, *boys*. The first thing I couldn't help but notice, though, when landing on the sun-kissed cement of La La Land, was that they certainly did grow them different out west...ignoring, as I tend to do, that I was on a college campus and the majority transplanted there just as I had.

My love of television translated into far deeper aspects of my life than just how I viewed dating and relationships: for years I had been dreaming about actually working in that field and *making* the television that would someday in the (near, I hoped) future shape another young child's life. When I moved to L.A. it was for the same clichéd reason you always hear: to work in entertainment. I started my career at a very small, very obscure campus television station called TV8 aka Trojan Vision, and that was where I met my first "real life" pin-up.

After my first few months volunteering at the television station, I was invited to be a station manager, which was a big deal for someone who had been working such a short amount of time, but an even bigger deal for a freshman. I happily accepted, noting that a managerial position not only came with a paycheck (meager as it may have been) but also the privilege of directing the live broadcast at least one night a week. And that was the goal from day one.

Somewhere along the way I also inherited some producing duties for the two entertainment news and film review programs our "little station that could" had to offer, and when the new semester started up, I had to attend casting sessions to find a new host or two for my shows. Maybe "had to" is misleading: with images of tall, equally sun-kissed wannabes and the few C-List ex-child stars enrolled dancing in my head, I eagerly used my position as manager to take on the responsibility of booking and running the casting sessions. Though we were taping each audition for show runners who couldn't be there in person and for reference later, I armed myself with a point-and-shoot digital camera, too...you know, *"for human resources."*[25] Sadly— or perhaps *luckily*, if you're not a fan of sexual harassment suits— I never got to whip that camera out, as the majority of those vying for an on-air hosting position ended up being women.

My Pin-Up didn't audition during that first round, though later when he did, a fight would break out between show runners who each saw a place for his gorgeous face on their show:

"But your show is a debate show, and he's a film student! Don't you think you need someone with a wider focus?"

"But he's so pretty!" would be the standard reply...well, maybe not aloud, but I'm sure they were all thinking it. Because I certainly was.

---

25 Once again, this is a quote from *Friends* when Rachel is enamored by a potential new assistant (Eddie Cahill) in "The One With Rachel's Assistant," Season 7, Episode 4, and decides to snap an impromptu Polaroid of him because he's "just so pretty." Needless to say, it *wasn't really* for human resources, and everyone *didn't* have to do it.

But I'm getting a bit ahead of myself here...

Typically during nightly broadcasts, we were in the studio for two hours, even if the better part of an hour was just sitting around waiting to switch a pre-recorded program on or off. It got to be such a routine that even with a skeleton crew of only three or four people in the booth, we were able to perform almost on autopilot. Occasionally I would even take to turning around in my chair, with my back to the monitors showcasing the frames of our cameras, and simply tell the technical director which shots to take by catching backwards glimpses of them reflected in the sliding glass door that allowed entrance into our control room. Yes, I had pretty much turned into a cocky, Kanye West level bitch at this point! And the night My Pin-Up first stepped foot into my control room just happened to be one of those relaxed, routine evenings.

In hindsight, though, it almost feels like fate that I wasn't running around like a crazy woman— as if the universe was telling me to slow down so I didn't miss the beauty that can be found in this world. That or the universe just wanted me to use the little taste of power that had so obviously gone to my head to my advantage and actually summon up the courage to make a stride in my personal life like I had been with my professional one.

At one point I was actually able to get up and walk to the back row to pre-approve the graphics for the next segment, and that's when the producer of the nightly talk show pulled open that sliding glass door. Now, he was a rather annoying kid, and arrogant in his own way—the kind of guy who was entitled enough to pull open a soundproof door in the middle of a broadcast just because he thought he *could*. I was all set to rip into him for the disruption, but then I saw whom he was toting behind him and decided it would better serve me to present myself as *some*what of a lady. Screeching at someone for being an arrogant @$$hole (even if that *is* what he was acting like) is no way to ingratiate yourself to someone cute... err, I mean, someone *new*!

My Pin-Up loomed over the producer, standing at over six feet to the producer's five-foot-eight hunchback,[26] who was babbling on about something nonsensical and gesturing around the control room as if he owned it. And looking back, he often babbled nonsensically but even more so when this guy was around; presumably *he*, too, would get nervous in the presence of such beauty. From the few rushed and slurred words I was actually able to make out, I learned My Pin-Up was interested in volunteering for the student-run television station, and somehow this producer had managed to rope him into *his* staff.

"For the time being," I smirked to myself, already determined, with just one glance at him, to snare him for my own show so we could spend time together in a forum in which I felt I had exceptional knowledge and skill, so he would be so impressed he'd realize he *just had* to get to know me better!

And for once—and perhaps surprisingly— that actually happened...to a degree.

I smiled and introduced myself quietly that evening, taking careful note of the way his tee shirt hugged his arms, the way the brim of his baseball cap was slightly worn, and the way his subtle hint of cologne smelled like the Drakaar Noir (or was it Curve?) of all of my childhood crushes. I slipped back into my chair and resumed my broadcast as normally as I could, even if I got periodically distracted by his reflection in my monitors, standing against the sliding glass door, watching intently with his arms crossed over his chest. I even "mixed it up a bit" with the shots, encouraging camera ops to change their framing to be a bit more film-like and stylized, and I switched between shots more often and faster than usual. So I was showing off a little; I wanted him to see a woman in control who knew what she was doing and wasn't afraid to take the risks.

---

26 Okay, he didn't actually have a hump, but by comparison, he might as well have...

Unfortunately in my personal life, though, I usually *do* give into fear and never take *any* risks.

My Pin-Up and I did work together a lot during the brief few years our educations overlapped. I managed to squeeze my way onto the crew of a show he hosted to spend extra time with him, though we also ended up in some of the same courses. Those were courses for which I (usually) actually showed up! All I really need is a little extra motivation...

All of my friends knew I "hearted" him, though I never said as much out-loud. And though I tried to act cool and like it didn't really matter, it was obvious how I felt from the way I'd look for him when I walked into the station or the way I would randomly bring up something he said while my friends had to endure my grinning like an idiot. I was in awe and in a lot of ways, still just that naïve, dreaming, innocent teenager.

Okay, I swear I'm not normally as shallow as I sound right now, but...oh screw it; he was pretty! And he was also a really good guy—very sweet and sensitive while still maintaining a sharp sense of humor. He'd hold doors open for me, which seemed rare in that day and age but even rarer in the location. College campuses—especially *my* college campus of USC—are known much more for the "gentlemanliness" of guys who make sure you never see the bottom of your red plastic cup at frat parties.

A friend once asked why, after I had finally admitted I had a thing for My Pin-Up, we simply remained friends. By "thing," by the way, I of course mean "obsessive crush during which I customized my ring tone so that every time he called, Mariah Carey's "When I Saw You" would blare from the speaker," so maybe that should say it all right there anyway.

In truth, I was the little sister or the "one of the guys" who he could talk to about other girls. No groaning is necessary; I knew just how bad that was while it was happening, but I was somewhat powerless to stop it. Hell, quite often this is *still* wants comes out of an initial attraction to a guy. I am much more comfortable relating platonically through real, grounded interests first than shoving my tongue down a guy's throat at a bar or party!

I know all too well that life is not often like it is on TV, so just because I "hearted" him didn't mean he shared such interest! But I also knew something much deeper was at play here, and it was the elephant in the room that I never spoke about—not even with my closest friends. See, I knew I liked the *idea* of a relationship much more than of what one actually consisted.

Here's the thing: I was young; I was healthy; I was in decent shape; but I was still entirely uninterested in sex.

I know, I know: it doesn't make any sense, right? If I were so physically attracted to the guy, why *wouldn't* I want to sleep with him? It wasn't just him, though; I wasn't interested in having sex with anyone. And I didn't want to start a relationship on false pretenses; I preferred to just worship from not-so-far-away, instead of complicating, or potentially ruining, the friendship we *did* already have.

Maybe I was just a wee bit asexual—like someone had been crushing Zoloft into my food consistently since I hit puberty—or maybe I was just uncomfortable with the whole nudity aspect. After all, I was knocked off my pedestal early in life!

When I was nine years old, my grandmother asked me when I was getting engaged. In many families, they probably would have just laughed the question off as the ramblings of senility setting in, but in mine, it was what passed as a serious question. After all, I was almost in the double-digit age bracket, and I had to start seriously thinking of such things or I could potentially find myself out of my teens and without a rock on my hand!

Later in that same visit to her home, my grandmother just sat by the pool, watching me swim in one of the first two-piece suits I ever donned, and when I pulled myself out of the deep end to dive back in once again, she called me over and told me, in her clucking tone, that I should suck in my stomach because, and I quote: *"The boys don't like the fatties."*

I assumed I was young enough— and not yet self-aware enough— back then to allow such a comment to roll right off my back right alongside those chlorine-filled droplets. And though somehow I managed to sidestep the kind of body image issues that could have led me to anything serious like starving myself, taking laxatives, or eating only grapefruit— although once in college I admit I tried the ice cream diet and actually lost three pounds that week— I have to note that it definitely fed my insecurities and never allowed me to delude myself that the extra roll around my waist was acceptable, let alone attractive.

So when it came to relationships—especially anything physical—I was pretty much as innocent as they come, even at my then already "old" age. And sure, the way I reacted to My Pin-Up had a lot to do with that: after all, the majority of the examples I had seen on television had been exceptionally chaste, eliciting a big "Ooo-*oooh*" every time the characters would simply kiss! Even in *Full House*, when Jesse and Rebecca conceived their twins, all we saw was a long, lingering, hands on the side of each other's faces kind of kiss in which one of them would lean back as the other was pressing his weight against her. But they always remained upright.

In the majority of the world of television with which I grew up, no one was having sex unless they were married[27]— and even then it was almost an event. Preparations were made ahead of time, and furniture was moved, at least in the *I Love Lucy* reruns on which I sustained during mornings home with a stomachache or sore throat. In reality I'm sure it was quite a different story.

27 I'm going to ignore *Melrose Place* here because it was quite clear— even for my young age— that *those* men and women were good for controversy but not much else, so I couldn't put too much stock into how *they* acted.

In reality I'm sure they were screwing like bunnies— tanned, toned, hairless bunnies...but for many years I didn't question it. It was just how life went: the evening ended at the door with a short, sweet, *simple* goodnight kiss. Sex was the one thing I couldn't learn about from television, it seemed— we didn't even have basic cable, let alone Skinemax! So let's face it: without having that example of what it's supposed to be like, I had nothing to teach me or ease me. So for anything more than a few stolen kisses, I couldn't possibly be ready.

Okay, so I guess maybe I wasn't really disinterested in sex, as I simply had no frame of reference. There I was: twenty years old, on the Dean's List at a prestigious, *expensive* university, living on my own, holding down a steady job successfully, and yet at this, I still reverted to the ways of a child.

Or maybe I have just been the definition of a "shipper" since long before even knowing the term existed. *Had* I known, I may have found comfort in the odd but vast community of those who cling to on-screen idols as much as I did. In actuality, though, I only learned of the term just a few years ago while reading an article on a fan press conference held to promote the *X-Files* sequel. A friend of mine wrote the piece and used the term so flippantly, I had to email her ask her what it meant. When she explained it was descriptive of those fans that are excessively emotionally invested in a relationship between two fictional characters, suddenly it all just clicked into place for me. *Of course* I couldn't I have any time or energy for a real, mature, *adult* relationship of my own! I spent all of it dwelling on, and holding inside the emotions from, countless others that seemed unfinished in my mind! There are only so many gaps an imagination can fill in, and considering I had been of the "seeing is believing" school for so long, I didn't necessarily feel that just because they may have sailed off into syndication, "happily ever after," didn't mean they still were or that *I* could be.

BATTERY OPERATED BOYFRIEND...

I hope what I am about to divulge is not taken to be too crass or crude to just plain T.M.I., but I feel I have to get it off my chest. For years I thought I was in control: though I didn't always choose to exhibit moderation with certain activities or habits, I always assumed that I *could*. And yes, I admit that sometimes to avoid allowing my addictive personality to take over, I just avoided certain things altogether, but I never truly thought I was prone to co-dependency. Not until I came across one very special electronic device, that is.

When I was looking to buy a townhouse— I couldn't find escrow on the map, but suddenly, somehow, I hoped to find myself there in my early twenties...and I really don't know where I got that from seeing as how my parents were content to live in a rent-controlled shoebox for almost thirty-five years of marriage. In fact, whenever my mother and I would play Monopoly, we'd inevitably give up about an hour in and call it a draw because neither one of us ever bought any real estate on that tiny little two-dimensional board, either, so there just seemed to be no point to the game.

But, as usual, I digress.

Anyway, when I was looking to buy a townhouse, I upgraded to a flat-panel HD television, and in doing so, had to upgrade my cable service in order to get the best quality picture for my money. When the Time Warner technician came out to hook up the cable line and configure my wireless Internet, he brought with him a very special friend. The "new" cable boxes being provided had built-in DVRs at no extra cost. Now, I had resisted getting

TiVo or any similar DVR (and *yes*, I know how odd that sounds for someone who prides herself on being a pop culture guru) not because I was technologically challenged—quite the opposite, actually: I learned how to use early Macs, playing game after endless game of Oregon Trail in the dingy computer lab in my elementary school. When the time came for me to take a typing test in junior high to see what level I placed at, I passed with one hundred percent and was rewarded with a free period instead of the secretarial class taught on mechanical desktop typewriters.

No, I was quite good with technology and electronics: I was always the AV geek (though we didn't have an official AV club in my junior high) who would have to hook up the VCR whenever we had a substitute teacher who opted to just show us movies instead of pick up where our real teacher left off.

I was leery of DVRs, though, because I saw them as the worst kind of parasitic, borderline abusive relationship: when you need boyfriend your boyfriend more than he needs you, and he knows it and perhaps emotionally and psychologically berates you for it, leaving scars only you can see but which are ten times harder to heal. Because while a DVR acts like it means well, and it's all about you, really all of the little, romantic gestures in which it takes part—if you step back and view it from an objective point of view—are *not*, in fact, charming but *do* consist of quite a few old-fashioned, semi-masochistic undertones.

A DVR tries to live up to the "thoughtful boyfriend" label they are so freely given in the media (ahem, *Sex and the City*; I'm looking at *you*!). After all, a DVR *does* remember what you watch and makes recommendations for what you might want to try, which I admit, might be nice…if it wasn't such a passive aggressive behavior. We all have the occasional moment where we don't want to have to think, and when our boyfriend offers to order our dinner for us, for example, we may agree. But the more it happens, the less it seems cute and harmless and more like someone is trying to control us.

The boyfriend, like the DVR, is basically saying he knows us better than we know ourselves.

DVRs have even been known to record an episode of one or two such programs, filling up *your* gigabytes with what *he* (yeah, I assume the device is male; who else would be so presumptuous to tell you what you like??) wants you to watch. I wouldn't be surprised if I came home one day to find hours of pre-game Monday Night Football coverage taped in the DVR's subversive way of making it look like it's for me (because I *did* try an episode of *Friday Night Lights* that one time) when really, he's just sick of constant female-centric programming like *Nurse Jackie* or *The New Adventures of Old Christine.*

A DVR often also makes you feel bad for missing an episode of your favorite show, much the way a boyfriend might make you feel bad for missing one of his softball games or cover band shows. It's such an easy machine to use how could you *not* record the show, after all? And once it's sitting there, waiting for you in your very own living room, why *wouldn't* you watch it? With the "old-fashioned" way of watching television (i.e.: linearly), you have to make choices. If two of your favorite shows are on opposite each other (let's use the upcoming Tuesdays at 8 debacle, when *The Biggest Loser* will be opposite *glee* and *No Ordinary Family*), you have to consciously pick one over the other; you have to act as an informed and responsible citizen. Maybe you'll catch up on the other show online the next morning, or during reruns in the summer, or maybe not even until it comes to DVD months later— or maybe you'll alternate weeks, watching one week of one and then one week of the other. Either way, though, you're limiting yourself to one show per time slot; you're using television in moderation and managing to hold onto some of your other interests and general sense of self.

I admit that it may seem like a benefit that with a DVR recording one show while you watch the other "live," you can get the best of both worlds, so to speak; you don't have to be a slave to network programming at all, and you can watch either or both on your own time. But who are we kidding— and this is the part where I should just stop the pretense of the general "you" and speak in first person because I am clearly only speaking from my own experiences and personality with how quickly I would get sucked into recording all sorts of programming I would never have even given a second glance without such freedom— suddenly the very device which was supposed to offer freedom from the shackles appointment television will be weighing me down in a different way.

Just like how in an abusive relationship, the abused comes to rely on the abuser for everything, often shutting others who "just don't understand" out completely, a relationship with a DVR has the potential to take a very similar dark turn. Not only would one suck me in with all of it's hip, cool features in order to make me rely on it for "all of my entertainment needs," but the device would undoubtedly turn me into a greedy, obsessive, Gollum-esque shell of my former self—one which has me clamoring to spend all of my time with my electronic counterpart and no one else. I'd become addicted to it in the most unhealthy, un*natural,* way, emerging from the warm, comforting electronic glow only to answer the door for the pizza delivery guy...who will undoubtedly be taken aback by my ashen skin, stringy hair, and dark, hallowed rings around my eyes. I would become a virtual prisoner, as the obsessive desire to suck up every second of time with my beloved inevitably takes over.

A DVR should be working while I'm out— assuming I can get out at all; in new relationships, it is said that you often spend most of your time curled up together in bed! I should be able to come home, plop down on the couch, put my feet up, and just relax with him. But just like "real" boyfriends who often disappoint in the amount they get done when not under your supervision, a DVR has the potential to cause more problems than it solves, too.

What about when there is a technical glitch that causes the DVR to skip a recording? Or when one show runs long, and the DVR isn't smart enough to compensate and keep it going so you miss the infamous final moments of a Very Special or otherwise super-sized episode!?

Suddenly all of the daytime programming that used to be reserved for housewives, unemployed people, and children home sick from school is fair game to be recorded; the compulsive desire to record every episode of *Ellen: The Ellen Degeneres Show* or *Live With Regis and Kelly*—just for the host chat, I'll tell myself (and you know what? Throw in *The View* for "Hot Topics" while I'm at it, since I *can*)—will take over and soon enough I'll be planted for the full hour (well, forty-four minutes with "blip-blooping" through commercials). It'd start by just wanting to see a specific guest, but it will spiral. Oh, it will spiral. The desire will become a need, and soon TiVo will be obese with episodes of *Judge Judy* and *Gilmore Girls* in syndication, even though you— oh, right, *I* already own the full series on DVD!

My ass groove will only sink lower and lower into the cushion as one hour will turn into two into three into four, and then in the blink of an eye, this behavior will have gone on for months, and I'm the zombie squinting at that pizza boy because the sliver of sunlight that streams in through the slightly ajar door is just too unfamiliar, and I'm rushing him out the door because my DVR is beckoning me back.

Now that I think about it, actions in such a relationship really mimic those of an addict, and the DVR is the drug-dealer who lets you sample his product to turn you into a junkie.

I don't cook, and I rarely bake anything but the pre-cut, pre-made Nestle Toll House dough I find next to the margarine in Ralph's. Any actual boyfriend I may have doesn't stand a chance of getting fat in my house, but my DVR? Well, that would be full in a manner of weeks, and even if I was past the "honeymoon stage" of wanting to stay at home and cuddle with it all day, I would very quickly find that I would *need* to— just to work through the erroneous shows stored in his memory so he doesn't experience capacity or functionality issues later. I'm sure I would settle into a neat little routine, but I don't think it would take me very long to start to resent it. Pressing the same buttons over and over may get the job done, but it takes some of the fun out of things, doesn't it? Bickering would ensue because I want to try new things, but the DVR is all tapped out, and the minute you throw the remote at it, much more than just his ego is bruised!

Since people now record programming to watch it at their convenience later, the ratings game has completely changed. Shows are pulled off the air prematurely because the number of viewers tuning in during its regularly scheduled timeslot is lower than ever. There is no sense of pride regarding favorite shows anymore; with a DVR, it's easy to take a show for granted—much the way some take their friends for granted when they're in a relationship.

I would stockpile episodes in my sleek, black box, assuming they'll always be there when I want to call them up. But maybe that date never comes or by the time it does, I get to episode three only to find that there is no four. Has my perfect mate experienced a technical glitch, like how he cuts off the last five minutes of *American Idol* when Ryan can't bring the show in on time (which, let's face it, is every damn week!)? Has he suddenly decided he's had enough of whatever shows and just rebelled by not allowing the presets to "take?" Or did the network pull the show because not enough people were watching? Could our selfish, self-involved relationship really affect that much outside of ourselves? DVRs have the potential to put more Below The Line crewmembers out of work than the 2007 WGA Strike! Not exactly conducive— let alone supportive— of my interests!

Love— and a relationship in general when it's bad— is like a drug: all consuming and with the capacity to completely screw with your head. So rather than risk becoming just another strung out lump, semi-comatose on the couch, mumbling to myself and scratching my arms, I have headed all of the early-nineties celebrities' advice (was I the only one wrote the D.A.R.E. hotline number down in my Hello Kitty address book and pretend Mark-Paul Gosselaar and I were old friends?) and just said no…to TiVo.

THE LONGEST RELATIONSHIP I'VE EVER HAD...

I'm going to come clean right now: I absolutely *abhor* weddings. And before you get all Judge Judy on me, I do not *abhor* weddings simply because I am single and "the event just reminds [me] of what [I] don't have" (as a particularly baffled acquaintance once accused me). I'm single, but that doesn't mean I'm broken. I'm not some sad spinster who prefers her cat's company to that of the opposite sex. Don't be stereotypical! I don't even have a cat; I have *a dog*.

No, I don't like weddings because I don't drink, and I don't dance, and I don't think it's fair to have to buy a salad spinner or crystal champagne flutes in exchange for an amuse bouche of salmon or chicken, a couple of shrimp cocktails, and a piece of overly sugary cake. Although I do love overly sugary cake...

And yes, I have always felt this way about weddings. In kindergarten one of the little boys in my class asked me to marry him, and though the adults standing around the schoolyard "Aw-ed" and "How cute"-ed at us, I stared him down and very flatly just told him: "*Hell* no!"

...Well, I *might* have added the expletive in later.

When that same little boy came up to me in the lunchroom in first grade and asked me the same thing again, I just rolled my eyes and walked away. Maybe he was holding onto the hope that he could wear me down— that eventually I'd give in— but that's not how my mind worked. He was a nice kid, but I had absolutely no interest in marriage— especially when he wasn't even offering the one nice perk of a sparkling, glittering, brand-spankin'-new piece of jewelry as my "reward" if I said yes. So I kept saying no. And eventually he got the hint.

Okay, sure, when Jesse and Rebecca got married on *Full House*, my then-best friend came over for pizza and soda and individual ice cream sundaes. I wouldn't let her talk unless it was a commercial, as I sat on the edge of my mother's plastic-wrapped loveseat, and pretended it was actually a wooden pew. When Zack and Kelly got married on the *Saved By The Bell* special made-for-TV movie, I invited a handful of my closest friends to partake in a slightly fancier reception. We had evolved past just pizza, and I put out an assortment of our favorite hors d'oeuvres: chips and dip, pigs in blankets, mozzarella sticks with marinara sauce, and freshly baked chocolate chip cookies. We got all dressed up, borrowed some of our mothers' makeup for the occasion, and watched our favorite couple take their vows with only forty percent jealousy that *she* got to marry Zack Morris, and we didn't.

And recently, I even teared up (though in privacy this time) at Jim and Pam's long overdue nuptials. Things were working out the way they were always supposed to— the way these shows had set up from the beginning— but if life was teaching me anything, it was that "Happily Ever After" never marks the end to anything but mere acts. There may be five acts to a life, just like there are five acts to a television show, and I knew there was plenty of more time to go.

My own mother admitted to me— although not until years later, when I was off living on my own and was old enough to get married myself— that she only stayed with my father because it was the easier, less expensive option. In New York, the fifty-fifty law is in place, which means that if my parents were to split up then, after thirty some odd years of marriage during which I can count on one hand the number of times I saw them hug or kiss or even smile at each other, they would have to divide everything down the line. Despite the fact that my father never held down a job or contributed to the household income in any way during that time. When I was a kid, he claimed he was "staying home to raise me," but even after I went to school, and then got involved in after school activities like swimming lessons and later theater, he still stayed home. He made his bed, and he quite literally laid in it every afternoon.

Splitting everything didn't seem so bad to me when I thought about it: they didn't own their apartment; they didn't own a car; they already had two TVs. Really the only thing for them to fight over would have been a bunch of worn-out VHS copies of Blockbuster movies (yes, we were old school pirates) and a brick of a laptop that really made a much better paperweight than communication portal. And besides, all of that is just stuff; it's just material. Freedom would have brought peace of mind.

Freedom. The mere fact that I was looking at divorce as something liberating should explain my feelings on weddings pretty loud and clearly.

When my mother got sick,[28] it became a different story, though. I lost my shit, panicking over how short life can be and how I couldn't imagine not doing whatever I wanted— and whatever I *needed*— in order to make myself as happy as possible. She, on the other hand, seemed to find comfort in the fact that this guy who made her scream and cry almost on a daily basis when I was a child was now still living there— albeit in a different room— to take her to the hospital or run out and pick up the Ensure shakes she suddenly needed to down in order to try to put back the weight she lost during her rounds of radiation.

---

28 Okay, to be accurate, my mother was *always* sick. She suffered from a genetic kidney disease that ended up taking my grandmother ever since I was a little kid, and she had to undergo a transplant when I was a teenager. Then came a bout with colitis. But when I say "she got sick," I am referring to her diagnosis with oral cancer. She was already in stage four by the time the doctors found it, and because she was still on anti-rejection drugs from her transplant surgery, her body was not fighting the tumor *at all*.

My mother and I never had the kind of mother-daughter relationship you see all the time on television, especially if what you watched was *Gilmore Girls.* I never told her about boys I liked; she never made me a dress for a school dance. To this day, I still don't even know much about how my parents met or what their ten years as a married couple were like before I came along. So, for all I know, maybe the simple act of him moving into a different room— my old room, to be exact— was enough to salvage a part of their relationship. And I've been to enough "therapy sessions" (read: babbling my problems incessantly to a friend over rolls of cookie dough and then having her babble her theories back only to switch roles just as deftly as we switch out the rolls of Nestle chocolate chunk for Pillsbury sugar) to know that if she found a way to make it work for her— regardless of how unhealthy it seemed unhealthy to me— no one would be able to convince her otherwise.

Who am I to judge how anyone else lives her life, though, anyway, right? I am the girl— err, excuse me, the *woman*— who still prefers to come home after a long day and watch five hours of television rather than grab dinner or a drink with a guy just for the free meal. I am the woman who, instead of heading my mother's "If you're in a bad situation, get out!" advice, just never puts herself in most situations...*just in case* they turn out bad.

I am a very particular person. I don't consider myself to be legitimately O.C.D.— and I've certainly never been officially diagnosed— but I would call myself "borderline." I don't have to flip the lights on and off in odd numbered sequences, carry wet-naps in my purse, or constantly run back home to check if I left my stove on (though maybe it would be better if I did do that last thing because I did have a gas leak for a day and a half before I even noticed; I am *never* in my kitchen!). But I have lived alone for so many years for a very specific reason. It is the same reason I have never hired a housekeeper for fear of turning into Murphy Brown when he or she inevitably put something back on the wrong shelf or just two inches too far to the left.

I like things a certain way, especially when it comes to the arrangement of the picture frames on my desk and dresser or the placement of the remotes on my coffee table. And though guys always find it endearing at first, "Aw, look, she has to line up her jewelry in a specific order before she goes to bed," eventually it grows to grate on them: "God damn, why is she so neurotic? Why can't she just drop it in a pile and come to bed already!?"

And it works both ways: where, in the beginning of a relationship I might be "cool" with doing all of the dishes the minute we finish eating because I know exactly where they go, after eating at my house a couple of times, I feel like he should be able to figure it out for himself and pitch in. It's the least he can do as a thank you for taking up space on my couch, eating my food, and forgetting to turn my television back to Fox KTTV HD before he turns it off (yes, just another one of my little "quirks;" I like to hear *Good Day LA*'s squawking when I flip it on first thing in the morning).

Needless to say, I am not the easiest person to get along with, and because of all of the years of back issues I had stored up, I never thought I would be living with a guy at all— let alone so soon into our relationship. But that is exactly where I found myself in the spring of 2007.

This story isn't exactly unique; you've seen it a thousand times before in a thousand different chick flicks: girl sees boy across a crowded room; boy smiles at girl; girl falls head over heels on the spot and runs to him. Only in my particular scenario, girl practically elbowed another girl out of the way to get to the boy they were *both* eyeing. And I certainly never thought I'd be *that* girl.

Madison Chandler[29] and I met in the Beverly Center. His eyes twinkled in the fluorescent light, and his salt and pepper brown hair

29 *Not* a nickname for once!

was like chenille between my fingers. We spent about twenty minutes getting to know each other in the back of a store that, unfortunately due to the slump our economy entered about two years after our encounter, no longer exists. Twenty minutes was all it took for me to know I wanted him to come home with me.

In the elevator on the way to the parking garage, Madison Chandler rested his head on my chest and drifted off to sleep, and any doubts I may have had about throwing down almost two months worth of rent on him went right out the window. He had me.

Madison Chandler and I majorly bonded from moment one— even though moment one had him heading straight over to my bookcase in the corner and peeing right in front of my collection of childhood photo albums. I was slightly annoyed, but minute two had me putting him directly in the bathtub so he would learn the lay of the land around my house. No boy— no matter how cute— is allowed to make a mess and get away with it! And it seemed to work perfectly; that first incident was his only one, and that is not an exaggeration. He had the quality that I wished every guy who came before him (and those who have been around since) could have adopted: he was easily trained!

I made his dinner that night, suddenly uncaring if it set up a precedent for his expectations of my domesticity. And I worked with him for days on end to teach him to live up to my standards: to sit when I wanted him to, to lay down when I asked, to give me hugs and kisses on command. He learned to close drawers on his own, to clean himself, and the names of all of this toys— not exactly the "a little to the right" that Jason's dog knew on *Gilmore Girls*, but it would do, and the LePaws Agency wanted to sign him nonetheless.

Madison Chandler learned to love the beach as much as I did, and I even compromised and agreed to take him on walks on the beach instead of just flopping down on my towel in the sand and reading or napping for hours on end. I began to share my snacks, and just as quickly my bed, with him.

I even got Madison Chandler to put all of his stuff away every night...but I was so proud of him for figuring that one out that I just kept buying him more and more stuff, and that little nightly ritual began to take over an hour. Eventually I figured it would be much more worth my time to spend that hour playing— or cuddling— with him rather than sticking hard and fast to my "rules." I may have been working hard to train Madison, but Madison managed to train me, too!

Almost a decade ago, I couldn't understand the logic behind why Monica on *Friends* was so upset when Chandler spoke out against marriage, calling it a scam from the government and "just a way for Big Brother to keep tabs on us." In truth, Chandler was really just trying to throw her off his scent, so that when he actually did propose, it would take her completely by surprise. But personally, I kind of saw his point. I mean, they were already living together; getting married was really just getting a piece of paper with their names on it— like a joint diploma in the school of relationships, I guess. Perhaps I saw his point, though, because it's been years and the only guy I can see spending the rest of my life with is of the canine variety.

Yes, Madison Chandler is a dog— a Shih Tzu, to be precise— but he's much more than the property that the law considers him. He is my child, my best friend, and the true love of my life. But as much as I love him, I have no desire to *marry* him.

About a year and a half ago, I almost got my chance to attend my second "full" wedding (ceremony *and* reception). It should have been a chance for me to turn around my views on the subject, except it would have been far from the happiest of occasions: one of my oldest, closest friends got engaged to a guy that I couldn't stand. Don't get me wrong, he wasn't a violent or dangerous guy; he didn't steal from her or try to hit on her friends or badmouth her family. He just never held a job for the year they were together, instead choosing to mooch off her, even to the point where she signed a few of his rent checks.

He was also co-dependent in the way that makes you understand why that word has gotten such a bad rap: he couldn't bear to be alone and would call and text her constantly throughout the day to see what she was doing or who she was with while he, inevitably, was draped over her couch, eating bowl after bowl of cereal, and probably smoking a bowl of a very different substance.

At first, she thought it was sweet. "He just wants to check in with me to show me how much he cares," she'd say.

"Or he's calling to check up on you to show you how much he can control," I'd counter.

She would usually just roll her eyes and change the topic.

Eventually he decided he didn't want to come to group outings anymore. And his neuroses wouldn't let her go out without him. "He just wants to spend the evening with some wine and a movie in bed," she'd say. "Isn't that romantic?"

That was when it was my turn to roll my eyes. "Or he doesn't want you to have friends or a life of your own anymore," I'd rebut.

Eventually she stopped talking to me about their relationship altogether. And the truth was: I liked it better that way. She already knew how I felt; we didn't need to rehash it, and I wasn't going to change my mind. I didn't want to make her feel badly about herself or her poor choice in men, and I *really* didn't want to hear her fawn all over what she called this guy's "brilliance," but what I was considered were just the ramblings of someone who spent too much time in an altered state.

In fact, when she called to share the news that she said yes to his proposal, my exact words were: "What? Why!??" I didn't blame her when she hung up on me then, but I was certainly surprised when she called me to apologize for it months later, after she called off the engagement.

"He wasn't exactly Prince Charming in the end, huh?" I asked her over Kung Pao chicken take-out that we ate around my coffee table, trying to avoid breaking out into the "Told ya so" dance I had been studying from Debbie Reynolds on my *Will & Grace* TV on DVDs.

"That may be the understatement of the year!" The woman, who had given up her rent-controlled apartment and moved fifteen miles north for the guy who turned out to be a giant douche nozzle, laughed.

"So you feel like you wasted the last year, huh?" I assumed with a slight shake of my head and a chuckle.

"Oh, no, not at all!" The woman, who had stood by the jerky guy even when he lost the dog she had had for *years* before he came along, exclaimed.

(And don't think I didn't wonder if he "lost" that dog on purpose, feeling threatened by the long-term history she shared with that other male in the house! He *was* that off-center.)

"No?" I just raised my eyebrow at her curiously, and she shook her head emphatically.

"Sometimes we have to make a mistake," she shrugged in that nonchalant way that only well-adjusted people know how to do. "How else do we learn?"

I just popped another bite of chicken into my mouth to keep myself from smirking...because we both knew how I haven chosen to learn!

SHE'S MAKING SOME CHANGES...

I somehow got tricked into helping my friend Kiki move semi-recently— if I remember correctly, I was lured there with the promise of endless Coldstone cupcakes— and as her son was on his second leg of his Guitar Hero World Tour in the living room, I climbed into the seemingly backless abyss that was her master closet, pulling out shoebox after shoebox for her to load by the half dozen into slightly larger cartons. As I slid the tenth or so across the floor to her, it suddenly dawned on me that I had never seen her wear so many pairs of shoes.

When I said as much aloud, though, Kiki just looked up at me as she tossed the next box in with the rest and told me that what I was handling with*out* so much care were not actually Jimmy Choos or Donald Pliners or from Nine West. Instead, the contents of the boxes were worth a lot more— on a sentimental level. The boxes were her boyfriend boxes. Why I didn't notice the guys' names in Sharpie scrawl across the sides of the boxes in the first place, I don't know.

Suddenly I flashed back: I had been here and done all of this before. It was a few years earlier, in a different part of town, and with a friend from college instead of the one who stood before me now. Only when we unearthed *her* boyfriend box that afternoon, she took one look at it, plucked a stuffed dog from its bowels, and told me to take the rest of it out to the trash.

"You know," I laughed at her, "you don't have to do *every*thing Rory Gilmore does."

On *Gilmore Girls*, when Rory and Dean broke up— for the first time: pre-Jess *and* pre-adultery[30]— Rory stuffed everything that even reminded her of the six foot three All-American "dimples" into a box and told her mother to throw it away. It included a sweater she wore out on a date with him (a sweater which was actually her mother's, if I remember correctly— and I usually do!), a book he saw her reading at the bus stop when they were first getting to know each other, and a stuffed rooster— Colonel Clucker!!— that sat on her chair for years prior to him but that he had said he liked when he first saw her room. Luckily for Rory, though, her mother had been through similar heartbreak in the past and had the good sense to just put the box in her closet for the day that Rory would once again want the items through which she could remember her first love.

Considering my friend from college's boyfriend had dumped her for someone he had started seeing while she was away on business, she was not amused by my comparison, though. She handed the stuffed dog to my own new puppy, who happily abandoned sniffing the ball of old jeans crumpled on the floor of her closet in favor of gnawing on it's plush head. Looking more pleased by this than she probably should have, my friend from college once again just told me to get rid of the box. I shrugged, and since I was not her mother or a person with spare storage space, I obliged.

"Be careful with that one," Kiki's voice snapped me back to present day, and I glanced down at the brown Ugg boot box in my hands. "It holds breakables."

Instead of soft suede and sheepskin boots, the box that had "Will" written on the side held about half a dozen small Kim Anderson figurines wrapped in paper towels. There was a little boy popping out of a trashcan holding a bouquet of roses, a little boy and a little girl sharing a milkshake, a little girl in a sunhat holding a giant heart, and a few more that were damn near identical. I raised my eyebrow and

30 Season 1, Episode 1: "The Break-Up Part 2".

caught her eye. "Will" was the guy who broke up with her because he realized he was gay.

Looking at the mountain of boxes that littered Kiki's bedroom floor, I couldn't help but think that my friend from college had the right idea after all. After a break-up, isn't it best to purge one's self of all of the things that remind you of the person who no longer takes up half your comforter or uses his socks to wipe up spills in the kitchen? (True story, by the way.)

But here Kiki was, not only holding onto old mementos of relationships she had no hope of (or interest in) rekindling but also asking *me* to schlep them over the hill to her new house. A house, I might add, that held no emotional tie to anything in her past and would only serve as the setting of many future (and hopefully happy) memories; why would she want to taint it with the remnants of once-deep connections that are now reduced to nothing more than a seven by nine capsule of time?

And just how far back would these boxes go? Did Kiki have the "Do you like me? Check yes or no" notes from elementary school or the piece of gum that got stuck to her retainer when she had her first kiss during a game of Spin The Bottle in sixth grade ("never happened")? Did she tuck the engagement ring from the last guy neatly alongside the restraining order she had to take out on him in end??

When I went home that night, still shaking my head at the ridiculousness that people hold onto (if you spend your time looking at old photos and trinkets and *reminiscing*, you're missing out on new experiences and memories you could be making by living in the moment!), I yanked open my own closet only to have a box slide off the top shelf and practically crash into my face like an unruly bobsled. The lid sailed off in mid-air, and the contents of this dusty photo box bounced swiftly onto the carpet, including a Playbill from the first time I ever saw RENT on Broadway, a copy of the very first soap opera magazine I ever bought, a shot glass from my first trip to Vegas when I filmed a behind-the-scenes at Cirque Du Soleil, the postcard on which Ashley and Mary-Kate Olsen misspelled my name when they were signing autographs at FAO Schwartz (to be fair, they were only six), etc etc etc. It was my very own memory box of sorts— only the items inside were not tied to memories of past boyfriends but instead important moments of pop culture in my life.

I sat down, cross-legged on the floor, and for the next hour or so began to do exactly what I had been mercilessly teasing my friend about only hours prior. I poured over each and every piece of my history with an ever-growing smile on my face as each one brought me back to a different time and place. There was the back to the director's chair that my mother bought me when I directed my first play in high school; it had my name and "Director" in white embroidered script on the faded black fabric. There was the Polly Pocket I used to carry in my purse when I went to my mother's office on school holidays— the one that she had bought me for my birthday in second grade but that I received a duplicate of the following month when one of my friends passed out the toy as a party favor for her own birthday party. There was the ID badge that marked me as a member of the *Ellen: The Ellen Degeneres Show* staff from when I interned there during my last semester of college— and which *still* got me free parking at Citywalk.

As I was packing everything tightly back into the box, getting ready to bury it behind enough old board games and coffee table books so no one would be the wiser that it was back there, something on my nightstand caught my eye: it was a leather bound notebook that I kept as part-personal journal, part-idea journal. I suddenly had the urge to stuff it, too, inside the box because I knew it also happened to hold about half a dozen ticket stubs from concerts and movies I had been to with the guy I was seeing.

Huh, that's a new development.

See, I've always been of the minimalist school when it comes not only to things of the past but clutter in general. My friend from college who told me to throw away her boyfriend box probably didn't realize it at the time, but she wasn't just acting out of anger at his infidelity but also years of my teachings. Every semester when she would pack up her dorm to head home for the summer, I would fight with her to just toss out the majority of the crap she had accumulated in the short four months. And every time she would yell back that no, she just couldn't bear to part with that corkboard full of old Mad Libs we filled out in CTCS 201, History of International Cinema. And she absolutely needed all of the crimson and gold buttons that said BEAT ____ (fill in whatever team the Trojans happened to be playing that week), even though she'd never wear them again and probably forgot they were even buried at the bottom of her underwear drawer (!?) until this very moment anyway.

Every semester, she'd eventually tire of taping up box after box (not to mention paying for the shipping!), and she'd give in and consent to trashing about a Glad bag full of random junk.

When I was packing up my own room to move out to Los Angeles, I didn't have a friend, let alone a Lorelai, with me to talk sense into what I took and what I trashed, so I ended up throwing away my middle school yearbook and the three-ring binder that held all of the photos of me and my friends from that three year period. I figured I would never really feel the need to reminisce since I hadn't seen the majority of the kids in those photos in the past four years even though we all lived within a mile of each other anyway. So it was just a pretty safe bet I wouldn't see any of them again after I moved three thousand miles west either.

You could say that memories were all I had, so I should have wanted to hang onto those books even more for that fact, but I was desperately trying to "zoom in as I burn[ed] the past to the ground," so I wasn't thinking along those lines.

All of a sudden, I had to wonder what the hell it said about me, then, that I was more interested in keeping a Pocket Mr. T (a keychain with six pre-programmed catchphrases from Mr. T—something a friend stole from the audience giveaway closet at *On-Air With Ryan Seacrest* when we interned there) and some random clippings from Entertainment Weekly than photos of the kids with whom I spent my formative years. After all, I had just spent the day slapped in the face with my friend's past conquests, which were all actually her own, and I was slowly realizing just awesomely askew my own priorities may have been. Hell, I was in the middle of this chapter when I looked up to see my cable box read "9:02" p.m., and I shrieked *"Life Unexpected!"* and promptly closed the lid of my laptop, losing my rhythm in the piece and not caring one iota. Yup, I know what's important in life!

As I flipped through the journal by the side of my bed, though, it became apparent that for once, what I was choosing to save had more to do with the experience— and the person I was experiencing it *with*. After all, the ticket stubs were for nothing revolutionary, opening night of RENT: The Broadway Tour starring Adam Pascal, Anthony Rapp, and Gwen Stewart aside! In fact, I didn't even particularly enjoy one of the concerts (sorry to the friend of his who we saw do an acoustic set at The Mint) or some of the movies (*not* sorry to Eastwood; *Gran Torino* was rank!). What made them worth saving this time around, though, was that each evening was an important one for us together, and for once, that was something I was genuinely looking to preserve. Did I mention this doesn't happen often?

The Scribe, as I have deemed him when discussing him with co-workers or friends from other circles who don't know him, and I met at Kiki's birthday party almost a year before the shoebox/journal incident. Kiki, who only knew him through a mutual friend anyway, was somehow still convinced we'd hit it off, and unbeknownst to me at the time, she only invited him to this intimate gathering so that she could "finally" introduce us. Apparently they had been at some party where everyone was playing "Pyramid," and his clues for Josh Charles included not only *Sports Night* but also more importantly, *Don't Tell Mom The Babysitter's Dead*.

I always said I wanted a guy who would be able to relate to, let alone understand, my references...I just never expected to find one who both "got" them and was actually straight!

So Kiki dragged The Scribe over to me the minute he slid through the door, gushing that I "absolutely [had] to meet this brilliant kid who is going to change the world with his screenplays." She may have been a little tipsy, but she wasn't completely off the mark.

Though I admit I just smiled politely at first when he held out his hand to shake mine and told me his name, I let him get me a drink and ask me questions about my own writing, which Kiki had already apparently told him all about. *Greeaaat.* So he was going to be the next Stephen Gaghan, and I wrote beach-reading chick lit; sure, that's a match made in literature heaven!

But the thing is: we did hit it off. We spent the next two and a half hours just talking alone in a corner of the party, and when friends would make their way over to say hi, we'd turn and smile and listen to the latest anecdote from whatever set they were working on but without offering much back, and they'd get the hint and wander over to the next cluster. We had more in common on a fundamental level than I usually found with guys in this town— let alone that I could usually learn in an initial meeting. We didn't just have the writing thing in common, but we were both approaching this business as artists first, worrying about bettering ourselves and our work and sharing a message, rather than focusing on success, fame, and profit— something which, especially after having gone to USC, I found *extremely* rare and therefore refreshing.

I saw The Scribe as being exceptionally grounded even though he was just as equally confident in himself. He had the air around him of "whatever will come will do so because it's meant to," and when he'd shrug things off, it never annoyed me that he wasn't being more aggressive towards what he wanted. His passion radiated, but he was comfortable enough to admit he was not in control of everything. He managed to put me at ease and bring me back down to Earth when my mind was racing a million miles a minute with my own goals and dreams and plans.

The Scribe and I began to hang out a lot after that birthday party, but always pretty casually and often even in a big group of mutual friends. Within a month, he ended up having to move to take care of his mother, whose own cancer flared back up at the time when my mother was first diagnosed. Some would say that the timing was off for us— that we were not meant to be because of the distance forced between us— but even I'm not that cynical. This was just another thing I found I could talk to him about that I didn't think anyone else would really understand.

We spent hours on the phone, chatting in hushed voices in the dark— well, I was in the dark; I can't say with first-hand knowledge where *he* was. We said things that we might not have been able to say otherwise— if we were actually face-to-face, watching the other's facial and body expressions react to our words. Again, or at least *I* might not have been able to say them in such a situation, especially considering I come from the blogging world, where it is really easy to hide behind a screen and modem lines. Each time I hung up, I felt my cheek burning from the heat radiating from my iPhone and wondered how time had gotten away from me so quickly. It could (and often *would*) be one or two in the morning, but I'd feel refreshed with the energy of a brand new day and just want to go out and do something, share something, or more importantly, *create* something. He brought out something in me that I had previously only experienced through particularly inspiring entertainment. But he was a real person, and even though he was not quite standing in front of me, it was still a bit new for me.

The distance thing actually worked for me. I was able to indulge in all of the "secret single girl" behavior to which I had grown so accustomed (like reading the newest issue of Entertainment Weekly in a hot bubble bath every Friday night) without feeling the pressure or obligation of always having to go out with the guy.

The Scribe moved back to L.A. six months later, after his mother thankfully took a turn for the better, and we celebrated our first official "date" after months of phone calls, emails, and Facebook chats by going to see the aforementioned *Gran Torino*. The movie itself may not have impacted my life in any great way, unlike some of those things I kept for years and years in my box, but the stub represented something deeper than just an event or trend for once.

As I told Kiki when she called the morning after her party, wanting to know what I thought: "He's exactly the kind of guy I'd want to be in a relationship with if I wanted to be in a relationship. I consider that *major* progress!

SOMEONE WITH WHOM TO EAT CHEESE...

No one has ever come right out and asked me if I'm a lesbian, but that doesn't stop me from sometimes wondering if they are wondering if I am one. After all, talk is cheap, and actions— or *in*action— speak volumes. The last "long-term" boyfriend I had was right after college; the time I've known some of my closest friends now has been one of perpetual singledom for me; and it most certainly *is* for lack of trying. I don't go out to clubs; I don't go out to bars; I don't have a profile on a dating website— unless you count MySpace, but you really shouldn't, and I haven't even logged in over there in months! It's not that I haven't dated; I've gone out on dates— I've "seen people," as the kids are calling it today— but even in doing that I rarely broadcast it. As Denise Richards likes to say, *It's Complicated*!

My life is an open book, but you first have to pull it off the shelf, dust it off, and open the cover before you can read all of the stories inside. In other words, when asked, I am always honest about who I am, where I've been, where I'm going, and what I want in life, but I don't always broadcast it without request (stop snickering!). I am a private person in addition to being a proud one.

When Miranda on *Sex and the City* gets set up with a woman at her law firm's company softball game,[31] she doesn't seem all that surprised. In fact, she almost approaches the situation— and the woman— with an "it was only a matter of time" attitude. As someone who was a dry witted, sometimes sarcastic, always cynical, and

31 Season 1, Episode 3: "Bay of Married Pigs".

severely driven single woman who tried to never get too emotionally attached to the men that flitted in and out of her life (should it be a surprise that she was my favorite of the girls?), she shrugged off the experience, saying of the co-worker who set her up: "He seemed so happy to have figured me out." It just seems to be so easy to assume that because she's of the gender that for so long relied on another to bring home a paycheck, fix the plumbing, and make all of the important household and life decisions, she can't possibly be able to function— or even happy to be— alone. There are too many people who are afraid of, intimidated by, or just plain don't understand women who don't feel the need to be in a relationship in every waking moment, so in some sort of twisted, narrow-minded logic, if there's no man in the picture, then there must be a woman.

I'm not a lesbian. Should I have stated that sooner? Have I left you hanging for a hot minute, thinking the true revelation of this story was finally about to be revealed?? But if I still believed in soul mates, I would think Liz Lemon was mine.

Liz Lemon (*30 Rock*) and I are kindred spirits of sorts: she once made excuses for blowing off an evening with her girlfriend, going out to a big industry event, and even a potential date— all so she could sit at home, eat a block of cheese, and watch *Top Chef*. Well, let's just say that I know that behavior all too well; in fact, I've kind of even gotten to the point where I stop making excuses, and my friends often stop asking me to do things on certain nights, based solely on what is on the television schedule. They have learned their lesson after too many past experiences of me flat-out saying that I preferred instead to just go home, eat a block of cheese, and watch insert-random-reality-show-usually-from-Bravo-here...though I do have a dog to hang out with at home, so I consider myself one step slightly above Liz because at least I'm not *alone* alone.

Also, unlike Liz, I have never fallen asleep in a pile of cheese...yet.[32]

---

32 Season 4, Episode 12: "Verna."

As head writer for the fictional *TGS With Tracy Jordan*, as well as being "besties" with G.E. executive Jack Donaghy (Alec Baldwin), Liz seems to have her sh*t together professionally, but personally she is a bit of a mess, as she only seems to attract losers (and not even the lovable kind), like a beeper salesman-turned-*Dateline* predator or the barely pubescent coffee delivery boy who still lives with his mom…or even the millionaire who pretended to be agoraphobic just so he wouldn't have to admit he was really under house arrest for fraud, racketeering, and arson. Though, but for the criminal record, the last guy seemed perfect not only for her but also for me. After all, he could provide the kind of relationship "[where] you don't have to try anymore, and you can just sit around together and goof on TV shows, and then go to bed without any funny business." Ah, to dream…

I once called a guy was dating "expendable"—not to his face, of course, but that doesn't necessarily make it any better. We had been talking about having children— not with each other but just in general— and I confided in him that I didn't want to have my own, biological children but rather adopt (again, just like my girl, Liz!). There are just so many deserving kids already out there who needed loving homes.

"Besides," I shrugged, "it's something I can do whenever *I'm* ready. I don't have to wait around to find the right guy to do it with."

Perhaps needless to say, he didn't take that so well. Instead of embracing me and praising me for being his own personal Angelina Jolie, he became offended that I would look at things in such a way. But for so long, I got so used to attracting only the guys in whom I wasn't interested that it was just easier to figure out a way to get what I wanted independently.

In college, I was already well on my way to becoming Liz Lemon (though I didn't know it at the time because there was no Liz Lemon back then to whom to compare myself) as a member of my campus television station. The summer after my freshman year, I stuck around to take extra classes to ensure I could graduate a year ahead of schedule and ended up making my rent money by degaussing tapes, rearranging the studio, and convincing incoming students to sign up to volunteer with us at their orientations. It was just me and three of my good guy friends in the office all summer, laughing, joking, and eating way too much Taco Bell than is okay for a lifetime. *We* invented the Taco Bell drive-thru diet! I would like my profit sharing check now, please!

One afternoon, my friend McLovin (and I use that nickname lovingly and only because he quite greatly resembles Christopher Mintz-Plasse, which we got quite a lot of mileage out of when *Superbad* was first released) and I hopped in his car to set out for our daily Gordita run. As we sat idling on the corner of W. 32nd and Figueroa, waiting to make the scary left turn, he nonchalantly mentioned that our mutual friend, and one of the two other guys in the office that summer— Guffaw, as I called him because of his very...uh, distinctive laugh— had a crush on me.

As McLovin turned the wheel and slammed on the gas, I let out a screech that rivaled his tires and unconsciously hit him in the shoulder, causing us to swerve just briefly into the oncoming lane. He shrugged, like it was no big deal, and told me he figured I already knew. After all, he and the other guys around the office had been singing "Little diddy 'bout Guffaw and Danielle..." to the point where Guffaw actually started humming along— though probably unaware that my friend had changed the lyrics a bit.

"Then why would you feel the need to tell me?" I exclaimed, already dreading the awkwardness that would await me when we arrived back.

Earlier that week, while cleaning out some of the graduating seniors' desks, I found a bag of condoms that had been tucked away after a promotion pitch went awry. They were supposed to get our logo printed on the wrappers, so they could be handed out with the tongue-in-cheek "A Trojan for a Trojan" slogan in order for the kids to think we were so witty and clever they just *had* to want to stick around to hear our full pitch. Or if nothing else, at least they'd put us on the map. As far as extracurriculars went, we had to compete with tailgating for the Pac-10 champ whose Q.B. had just won the Heisman, after all.

Suddenly it made a little more sense why Guffaw was staring at me so hard when our third friend dared me to taste the cola-flavored one. I really don't want to know what the janitor thought when he was emptying our garbage cans that evening, but he wore a smirk on his face when passing us in the hall the next morning. Apparently even *he* knew.

Now, I don't mean to sound like an egomaniacal narcissist, but I can't figure out why this guy would think I would consider going out with him. It's not that I thought I was better than him— he was actually a really nice guy— but we really had nothing in common. He was into biking, football, Big Bear to actually ski and snowboard, and video games. I…uh…was not.

Guffaw also took it upon himself to begin "checking up on me" around the station. There was a couch in the corner of the office, next to my desk, and I would often come in to find Guffaw lounging on it casually, as if he was waiting for me. McLovin liked to make jokes that he was trying to create a "love den," but I wasn't laughing. I was desperately trying to figure out a way to keep it from getting awkward. But unfortunately, all that meant was that I was suddenly über-aware of myself. If I laughed a joke he told, was I sending him a signal that I liked him? And on the flip side, if I go out of my way to talk about the guy on whom I *did* have my eye, was I a giant bitch?

There was another guy at the on-campus station whose eye I apparently caught at one point in my tenure there. He liked to carry himself as "an executive," preparing himself for the lush, comfortable, conservative, formal, and *important* lifestyle he was determined to create for himself. In fact, if I ever do sue Tina Fey for ripping pages out of the book of my life to create her show, I am citing this guy as the inspiration for Jack Donaghy.

Pancake, as I deemed this producer because of how flat his face was, thought that what made him important was his college alma matter, social status, car, and the fact that he wore Armani suits—even to places where said suits made him stick out like a sore, spoiled thumb. He even had an embarrassing collection, not of cookie jars but of gaudy, brass USC paraphernalia! It was in the days that I had to contend with him that I developed a serious "eating just to keep me from saying anything too insulting" problem, stuffing my face continuously when cameras were rolling, and when they weren't, with donuts and pizza from the Craft Services table.

Pancake was the exact spiritual opposite of me, and yet he, too, thought we would stand a snowball's chance in hell as a couple. Or maybe he just wanted to get laid. How little he truly knew about me, right??

Pancake's way of enticing me to go out with him was by telling me that he had a hot tub back at his apartment, and we could watch the Super Bowl while "drinking some beers and taking a soak." Clearly, he had not gotten to know me, nor my interests, *at all.* Though I guess I should have been somewhat flattered that he thought I was attractive enough to be considered a "trophy girlfriend?" I don't know; putting a positive spin on an uncomfortable situation has never quite been my strong suit!

A few years later, I took a job in a corporate office, where there were only two guys worthy of even "eye candy" status. One turned out to be gay, and the other— well only three or four minutes into our first conversation he had already mentioned his girlfriend, so I resigned myself to the fact that there would be no interoffice flirting going on— probably much to H.R.'s delight. Well, at least there would be no flirting on *my* part.

Only a few months into my new job there, I took on the task of working with another department on an upgrade to our asset tracking system and apparently caught the eye of guy heading up the development team. From then on, he had a habit of walking up and down the rows of cubicles, peering over the top, to see if I was at mine. My co-workers liked to joke that whenever our new upgrade was experiencing glitches, it was just his way of creating a reason to talk to me. Now, none of this would be a big deal except for the fact that he was the kind of socially awkward guy who didn't seem to have a filter that told him when to use tact or to just plain hold back because the commentary is irrelevant, let alone unwelcome. He was kind of like an unfunny version of Frank Rossitano, but being Frank's boss, Liz Lemon got to tell *him* when to shut it. I could only sit back and pretend not to notice his creepy "loner guy at a teen movie" vibes.

There was also the guy I called expendable, who to be fair, I was actually quite into at first. Unfortunately I quickly learned he liked to do everything in an over-the-top way, and when I told him of my desire to adopt, he took it to mean that I was secretly testing him to see if he was as serious in this relationship as he assumed me to be: he took it to mean I wanted him to do something to prove he could be a good father. He was an "actor," in the sense that he shot a lot of no-budget five-minute scenes for YouTube with his friends but never really had a "real" gig...or a real job. I think his mommy and daddy were still paying some of his bills, and that alone was too big of a turn-off. You can't call yourself a grown ass man if you can't support yourself!

He didn't just do things exaggeratedly, he also did them somewhat skewed. When he realized I seriously thought about having children, he still didn't think it might be a good idea to try to buckle down and either take some of the modeling work he claimed he got offered ("But that's not true acting if my voice isn't being heard." Um, okay...) or at least get some sort of steady, part-time "regular" job to fill the time between the auditions on which he claimed he was going. No, instead he decided it would be a good idea to "offer" to move in with me.

At first I assumed he was kidding, and I laughed in his face, which turned out to be the absolute wrong reaction.

"I'm serious," he pouted. "Think of all of the money we'll save by splitting the bills."

Read: Think of all of the money *he'd* save by moving into *my* apartment.

I gained my composure, though, and stifled the nagging voice in my head telling me that I was the one who wanted a child, and here he was, selflessly offering to give me just that. I could come home from work to find Oreo crumbs across the coffee table, empty Coke cans littering the carpet, and a Playstation hooked up to my new flat-screen. And at least he was already potty-trained, right?

...Oh yeah, and then there was also the guy who told a bunch of my friends we were dating even though we had never even so much as drunkenly made out at a party. He created elaborate lies about our "relationship," somehow convinced it wouldn't get back to me— or perhaps he hoped it *would* get back to me and I'd run to him, saying I wished they were all true and we'd live his version of "happily ever after." He concocted some story about taking me on a picnic at the Getty Center, and I haven't been able to look at wicker baskets or checkered cloths since!

I know, I know: I'm *such* a romantic!

Unlike Liz, I have never gone on a date with a woman,[33] though if these were my primary choices in the way of "suitors," then maybe it would be better if I did! These guys were only offering me a glass ceiling in their world, but if the Spice Girls taught us anything, it was that when strong, individual females got together, their combined powers could be more than impressive! And somehow the Jack Donaghy type of behavior wasn't so funny when I was immersed in all of it, day after day, instead of just watching it play out on a forty-two inch screen in front of me, twenty-two minutes at a time.

33 Season 1, Episode 3: "Blind Date".

I should probably come out and admit I am an addict, and television is my drug of choice. Is this too little, too late? Please spare me the "Well, *duh*" that you might be thinking. They say the first step to recovery is to admit you have a problem (though I've never really been sure of who "they" are anyway), so there it is. When I find something I like, I cling to it like it will be stripped from me at any minute. I hungrily devour all of the information about it I can— obsessively flipping through magazines in the supermarket checkout line, consistently typing it into search engines online, whatever it takes, really. It is something that I can only equate to the way someone who has grown up poor feels when they finally start making decent money: they are acutely aware that it can all be gone in an instant, and they fear that more than anything so they hoard as much as they can. For so long I struggled to find an outlet, and I just didn't know what would happen if it was taken away from me. Sometimes that outlet has been a show, sometimes a subject matter, but sometimes still it is a person, an actor or writer or director…or even a character.

I guess in reality, I seek out people who seemed to be like me— in personality, beliefs, background, and interests— and who have all that I wanted to have, too, because I need some sort of validation that it is all okay…or more than okay: that it is actually obtainable.

I was always creative— an artist of sorts— but I came from a family who believed nothing lucrative would ever come of such outlandish dreams. My actual relatives would roll their eyes at me in the *"Oh, that kid!"* sort of way that exhibited they didn't take me or my dreams seriously. Eventually they stopped sugarcoating altogether and just told me to "get [my] big head out of the clouds!"

There wasn't anyone in my immediate life growing up that I saw as like me in those ways or who were in the position I wanted to be in at their ages, so there was no one in my immediate life to go to for advice or guidance. I was on my own with the glow of the set-top box.

I go back and forth on any given day from considering myself severely stunted by such reliance on television to teach me the ways of the world to thinking I was extremely lucky to be able to learn from experiences through said box instead of having to go out into the real world and make my own (detrimental) mistakes. Sometimes I think a part of me will always be stuck in a perpetual state of adolescent immaturity— *"eternally twelve,"* if you will— clinging hopelessly and desperately to something that isn't quite real because of the traditionally passive activity to which I devoted my life. But those were the experiences that shaped me into the woman I am today, even if they were ones simply viewed from afar, almost voyeuristically. Sometimes, most literally, what we see is all we know.

Besides, just because I don't *need* a relationship to define me or make me happy doesn't mean I'm entirely closed off to one if the right guy should come my way. So Jensen, if your current marriage doesn't work out, feel free to call!!

I TOLD YOU SO.

ABOUT THE AUTHOR

Danielle Turchiano is a freelance Writer/Producer who has worked on over a dozen independent film and television projects and self-published her first novel in November 2007. She is a self-proclaimed pop culture addict who contributes to various online entertainment news sites in addition to owning and operating the blog (of the same name) upon which this book is partially based. There the tagline reads "so much television coverage it may make *your* eyes bleed! Until she gets her own television show, or this book becomes #1 on the Best Seller list, she may consider that her crowning achievement.

Don't think that just because she is older, Danielle Turchiano no longer gets her life lessons from TV! This book may have told tales of her formative years, but the obsession most certainly continues; she just no longer gets *all* of her lessons there. Now she also learns from her favorite furry little guy, her dog Madison. Hmm maybe a sequel memoir will have to be in the works…

Danielle and Madison live in Los Angeles CA where they also enjoy cupcakes and the beach. For even more pop culture ramblings, you can visit her blog at www.possiblebypopculture.com and/or follow her on Twitter as @danielletbd.

Breinigsville, PA USA
04 April 2011
259100BV00004B/84/P